The man attracted her, but he was a Carmody

"In case you don't know it, Mr. Carmody, the property line between our farms is that little brook. The other side of that brook, to be specific."

"Why that's wonderful," he crowed. "You don't change a whit, do you? You're every bit as mean in the morning as you are in the afternoon!"

"Every bit," she assured him. "Now, if you've got something important to do, don't let me keep you."

"Nicely put, Kitty. I—"

"Miss Anderson, please."

"Say, I was wrong, wasn't I?" He was wearing a decrepit ten-gallon cowboy hat. He took it off and wiped his brow on his shirtsleeve. Kitty was too curious not to bite.

"You were wrong?"

"Of course. You're meaner in the morning."

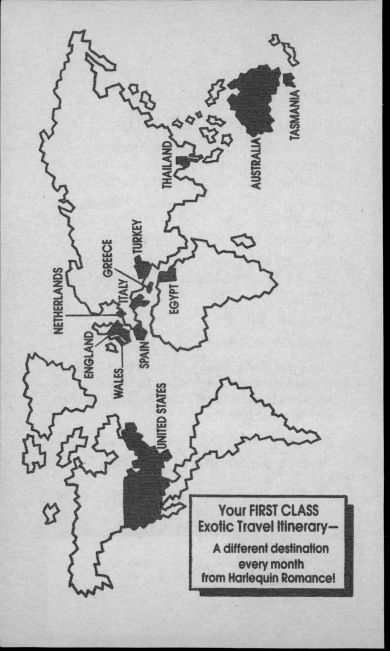

A TOUCH OF FORGIVENESS

Emma Goldrick

Harlequin Books

TORONTO • NEW YORK • LONDON
AMSTERDAM • PARIS • SYDNEY • HAMBURG
STOCKHOLM • ATHENS • TOKYO • MILAN

Original hardcover edition published in 1990
by Mills & Boon Limited

ISBN 0-373-03164-5

Harlequin Romance first edition December 1991

A TOUCH OF FORGIVENESS

CHAPTER ONE

NORTHPORT was not the largest town in Massachusetts, but neither did they take in the pavements at sunset. Set in a triangle south-east of Fall River, south-west of New Bedford, several thousand miles west of London, the village which was the town centre boasted a small supermarket, VFW Hall, Botworth's drug store, and the Northport Savings and Loan Bank.

Kitty Anderson parked her ten-speed bike in the little rack up on the boardwalk and looked grimly around her town. Four little boys were playing kick-the-can in the street just in front of her, and the can rattled to a stop at her feet. With perverse intensity she booted it clear across Main Street, and glared at the boys. A young man much older, perhaps in his middle twenties, returned the glare. She thought she knew him. The banker's son?

'Old grouch!' one of the boys yelled at her pretty little back as she picked up her sack and stomped into the bank. If they had been a little older they might have commented on her trim five-foot-two-inch figure, her Swedish-blonde hair, the tiny breasts that just would not grow to match her twenty-five years. If they had been a little closer they would have run at the anger in her deep blue eyes.

The two old men sitting back in the shade followed her, shaking their heads. 'Used to be the sweetest little girl in town,' the bald-headed one commented.

'Yeah,' the other replied. 'Until her brother lost his share of the land and run off. Can't imagine how such a stubborn woman could have had that wimp for a brother. Since she come home to run what's left of the farm she ain't spoken a single sweet word, that one.'

'Shouldn't be surprised,' Baldy answered. 'Workin' herself almost to death. Shame!' They both shook their heads and went back to their checker game.

The people inside the bank reacted to those eyes as Kitty stormed in. Male customers smiled at the challenge; females nodded approval of the determined little chin and squared shoulders. Bank employees, all of them, ducked, or tried to find some way of appearing busy. Kitty paid them no attention, but strode across the lobby to the one desk that represented the loan department.

'Good morning,' Mr James Randolph said uneasily. He shifted his rotund figure in his chair, unconsciously pushing himself an inch or two away from the girl.

'Some might think so.' She slammed her sack down on the desk top. Her eyes defied him to say something, but he refused the gambit. 'I've come to pay off the loan,' she said. Her voice was a deep contralto that carried across the room. The husky red-headed man standing in line at the teller's cage turned around to study her.

'I—I'm sorry about all this,' Mr Randolph stammered. 'We in the bank were——'

'Crooked as a snake's belly,' Kitty snapped. 'You bamboozled my brother just to get your hands on the beach-front land! And now you're sitting here licking your lips, hoping I couldn't come up with the mortgage money on the rest of the farm. Well, I'm sorry to disappoint you!' She didn't sound the least bit sorry, and the banker kept a close eye on her, as if she might be packing a pair of pistols.

'But your brother gave us power of attorney, Kitty. We were as surprised as you were when——'

'When the guy you sold half that land to turned out to be a fly-by-night mass-market developer when my brother expected him to build a summer camp for the city kids? Well, let me tell you, *Mr* Randolph——' she emphasised the 'Mr' so strongly that he winced again '—you don't have to live across the street from six rows of identical little cottages, each with their own swimming area and cesspool. Which have managed, by the way, to pollute my only well! It's been a long time coming, but I'm going to take care of you all—believe me, I am! How much do I owe you?'

The banker cautiously opened his desk drawer and pulled out an accounting sheet. 'Five thousand six hundred and fifty dollars,' he said. 'The bank will waive the sixty-two cents.'

'Don't do me any favours,' snapped Kitty. She turned her sack upside-down and spilled piles of currency across the desk.

'All five-dollar bills? I'll have a teller count it with our machine.'

'I wouldn't trust your teller or your machine to count the laces in my shoes,' she said. 'It's all legal tender, isn't it?' The banker nodded helplessly. Kitty picked up the nearest bundle and began to make a stack in front of him, one bill at a time. Although the air-conditioners were fighting off the August heat, Mr Randolph was perspiring madly.

When they reached the one thousand mark he pushed his chair a little further back and stood up. 'Look, Kitty——'

'Miss Anderson, if you please.'

'Look, Miss Anderson. We trust you implicitly. There's no need to count the rest of the money.' Katherine Lucy Anderson looked him up and down as if he were some species of worm just crawling out from under a rock.

'That's not what you told my brother,' she snapped. 'He was short what? Two hundred and sixteen dollars out of six thousand. And you foreclosed, you miserable—banker! We'll count it all, even if you have to miss your lunch!'

And they did. Every miserable dirty bill, each piled on top of the next with care and attention, as Mr Randolph became more and more glassy-eyed, until it was finished. 'Now you'll make me a receipt, stamp the loan papers "Paid" and——' Kitty watched, fascinated, as one of the piles of bills began to totter. Mr Randolph made a mad grasp and missed. The pile shifted, was caught in the steady pressure from the air-conditioner system, and went floating away, one bill at a time. One of the female customers squealed. A little girl, hardly two, sat down in the middle of the floor and gurgled as the five-dollar 'aeroplanes' sailed around her in all directions.

'Help,' Mr Randolph said weakly. And then, like a fog-horn blast, *'Help!'* Customers and employees all came to a halt. The air-conditioners redoubled their efforts. Bills floated up towards the ceiling.

'Help me, Kitty!' Mr Randolph wailed.

'Stamp the loan paid,' she demanded.

There had to be something about floating money that excited a banker, made him lose control of his senses, no matter what the denomination. 'Stamp the loan paid,' she said again, and he fumbled on his desk for the right stamp. Kitty snatched the paper out from under his fingers as soon as the stamp was affixed and initialled.

'Well, *now* help me,' the banker muttered.

'Not me,' Kitty returned, smiling. 'It's not my money now.'

'Damn you, Kitty Anderson,' he groaned as he fell to his hands and knees trying to scoop up the volatile money.

'Probably,' she replied, enjoying the scene. Maybe it makes up a little bit for the anguish my brother felt, she thought. Just a little bit. Maybe it makes up a little bit for driving Robert out of the town where he'd lived all his life. Maybe. Or maybe I'd like to see the whole town grovelling. All the little miseries she had suffered during the past year, trying to pay off the bills, restore the Anderson name, all of that started to pour out of the sides of her mind, as if a huge container marked 'Hate' had sprung a leak.

She felt like screaming at them all, but that tiny ball of good memories buried under the hate was touched by something else. The little girl had captured two bills, and was doing her best to eat them. In the back of her mind Kitty heard her mother's voice: 'It shouldn't hurt to be a child!'

Her reluctant feet carried her to the centre of the floor. The child looked up and smiled, the money projecting from both sides of her jaw. 'Shouldn't eat that,' said Kitty as she stooped to do something about it. She failed to notice that the red-headed man had come just as swiftly as she, bent at exactly the same time as she. Their foreheads collided with an audible thump. 'Oh, lord!' Kitty Anderson sighed as she collapsed backwards on the floor, cracking the back of her head on the tiles.

Perhaps only seconds had passed. Or minutes. Kitty blinked her eyes and tried to look around, but it hurt to turn her head. Customers were still chasing bills in the air currents; Mr Randolph was exposing a very large and naughty vocabulary. And Kitty's head was resting in somebody's lap.

'Who——?' she gasped as she struggled to sit up.

'Take it easy.' A vibrant deep male voice. 'You've got bumps both in front and back, little lady. I'm sorry.'

Kitty probed at her forehead, where a considerable swelling was located, then gingerly felt the back, just above the nape of her neck. Another bump. There was hardly any pain, but her mind was not exactly settled. She felt a strange mirth, a light-headedness, a flighty feeling she had not known lately. This man seemed to surround her—oh, not with just his arms, but with the whole aura of his maleness. 'Well,' she said wryly, 'my father always said I'd fall hard for some man some day, and be in a lot of trouble.'

'Atta-girl,' he said soothingly. 'Some knock! I'm afraid I had my eyes on the baby, instead of watching what I was doing. Think you could stand up?'

'Why?'

'Because——' he started to say, then laughed. 'You do my heart good, lady,' he chuckled. 'Why? Exactly. If you feel like sitting in the middle of the bank lobby for a while, why not?'

'I'm not a lady,' she grumbled. 'Being a lady doesn't pay. Not in this town, it doesn't! Where's the little girl?'

'Right at your elbow.'

Kitty managed to turn her head a degree or two. The child was standing solemnly at her father's side, watching with big green eyes. Her hair was red too—not the sandy red of the man, but rather a darker russet that gleamed and sparkled. Her little heart-shaped face made her look like a doll until she smiled. She sported a complete set of tiny little pearl-teeth. Not the 'cute' type of little girl, just a wholesome young thing with a nice smile.

'Hello,' Kitty essayed politely.

The child stared at her, then back up at the man behind her. 'Mary Margaret,' he said, and his voice was a gentle caress, 'I'd like to introduce you to this nice lady, but I don't know her name.'

'My name is Katherine,' Kitty said. 'Although most people call me Kitty. I'd shake hands, but I'm afraid I'll fall over if I do.'

'Kiss,' the child said firmly, and proceeded to do just that.

'She likes you,' the man said, smiling. 'Not many she likes. My name is Joel. Do I get to kiss you too?'

'Down, Buster!' snapped Kitty. Her eyes were beginning to focus. He was really an interesting-looking man. A shiver ran up her spine. Not handsome, not at all, but—interesting. His red hair was thick and short, his face wide and sun-scarred, as if he spent most of his days on the water. His nose was just the slightest bit—disarranged; it wouldn't be polite to say over-large. There was something about him that intrigued her. And green eyes, like the child's. His daughter?

She sat up, breaking away from his arms, and he turned her loose almost regrettably. 'Don't you think your wife will be looking for the pair of you?' she asked. He grinned, as if he knew the ploy.

'I don't have a wife,' he said.

'But—the little girl——'

'I like women who have a bump of curiosity,' he interrupted.

'Well, I've got all kinds of *other* bumps today,' Kitty mourned. 'Why not curiosity?'

'Why not?'

He shifted his weight and stood up. Not the tallest man I ever saw, Kitty told herself, but *tall* is a comparison. He must be five foot ten or eleven—something like that. And to a five-foot-two-inch girl any man over five seven was a giant! He extended both hands in her direction. Without thinking, she tucked her little hands into his, where they promptly disappeared. One gentle tug and she was on her feet.

'Help!' screamed Mr Randolph. The officious banker-person had disappeared, and he looked like an over-weight elderly man looking for a heart attack.

'Wait here,' said Joel. He walked casually over to the wall, flipped the air-conditioner switch off, and watched with a satisfied look as the bills began to flutter towards a landing. 'You're welcome,' he told the awestruck banker.

'Now then, Miss Katherine.' He tucked a hand under her elbow, used the other to latch on to the little girl, and headed them towards the door.

'Kitty,' she insisted as she moved reluctantly under his urging. 'My friends call me Kitty. Or Kit. Where are we going?'

'Kitty? Nice. We have a number of things on our schedule, Kitty. But first—although I've only been in town a couple of days, I know that they do a mean banana split over at the drugstore. I owe you. Now don't tell me you're on a diet?'

'Lord, no,' Kitty admitted. 'Double scoops?'

'Sure.'

'Chocolate syrup?'

'Why not?'

'Almonds?'

'Hey!' he protested, laughing. 'Anything that turns you on, including a maraschino cherry. What do you say to that?'

'It's beginning to look like a nice day,' Kitty responded with a grateful sigh. 'Good morning to you both!'

Botworth's was not crowded, despite the noontime hour. In fact there was nobody at the ice-cream counter, two people at the prescription counter, and about six at the lottery counter. So Kitty sat down to the split of her choice, having added pineapple chunky syrup to the chocolate sauce. Little Mary was settled in a child-seat, thoroughly strapped in, 'because she's not quite sure where her mouth is,' Joel explained.

'So now,' said Kitty as she came up for air, 'you were going to tell me about Mary's mother.' Why it seemed to be so important a question she could not remember, but it was!

'Oh? Was I?'

'Indeed you were. If you didn't downright say it, you at least intimated that you would. I hate a welsher!'

Almost automatically Joel had picked up the child's spoon and was feeding her from a smaller single-flavour dish. When the spoon came too slowly or too infrequently the child would bang on her tray and grin.

'Now, about Mary's mother?' Kitty persisted.

Joel shook his head. 'Dead,' he reported. 'A car crash, when Mary was barely three months old.'

'Oh, lord—I'm sorry. I hope I didn't bring back bad memories. I know how that can be. And you raised the child by yourself? Not many fathers have that sort of courage.'

'I'm not her father, I'm her uncle.'

'Nuncle,' little Mary gurgled. 'Nuncle Joe.'

'Not going to say anything else?' he asked as Kitty dived back into her banana split.

'Not another word.' She sighed for all the things she wanted to know, but dared not ask. 'I can't eat my troat with one foot in my mouth.' And I think all the usual words wouldn't fit this man and his circumstances, Kitty thought as she studied his face out of the corner of her eye. Phlegmatic? Was that the word for a man like him? With all his troubles unfolding, his face was as calm and as distant as the ocean horizon on a clear day. A tough but tender man?

'So I'll tell you anyway,' he decided. 'Mary is the daughter of my brother Frank and his wife. They're both dead. Although I'm a bachelor, the Family——' he said it that way, with a capital letter that could be plainly heard '—the Family decided I ought to take charge of the child.'

'It must have been difficult. Hey, I'm not into that mother-love stuff or family care, but even an outsider would see how difficult it must be.' The baby grumbled. Kitty picked up the spoon and made a passable first attempt at feeding her.

'Not at first,' he continued. 'When she was just a little bundle that smiled and burped there was always somebody I could hire to take care of her while I went off to work. But now that she's become more mobile— well, obviously something has to change. Which is why I came back to Northport to think things over.'

Watch it! The little alarm light in the back of Kitty's head lit up and blinked in headlines: 'Bachelor Father Seeks Child-Care Assistance!' Whose help? Any presentable female he could latch on to! Another of Kitty's little fallacies. She looked on herself as a 'presentable' female, paying no attention at all to the dozen or more young men who considered her to be very much more than passable! Very carefully she put the spoon down and folded her hands in her lap.

'Yeah, well, I wish I could help you,' she stammered, 'but I'm not into child-care and toddlers. I'm not against it, you understand. I recognise that the world needs children and all that, but not mine. I just don't have any qualifications in that line!'

Joel straightened up and laughed, a booming cheerful sound that filled the shop. 'You handled that spoon with a great deal of skill, Kitty.'

'Probably. I've been eating for twenty-five years.'

'That long? I would have guessed nineteen. No, I didn't mean your spoon, I meant Mary's.'

'Boy,' Kitty muttered under her breath, 'what some men will say just to get their own way!' But there was a nice sound to it, wasn't there? Only nineteen? Sweet nineteen and never been kissed? Ha! If only he knew how close he was to the truth. Sweet twenty-five and hardly *ever* been kissed! Come on, Kitty. You're putting words in his mouth as well as your own! Change the subject.

'It doesn't seem to be hard, feeding the kid,' she said. 'I've had no practice at all, you understand, but—well, you know, the movies and the TV and all, you can't help picking up an odd fact or two. Hasn't the weather been lovely this week?'

'Yes, lovely.' He was laughing again, and it was infectious. The little girl began to bang her spoon on the tray in front of her, giggling away madly in time with her uncle's contortions. Kitty managed by might and main to avoid smiling. It was hard. In fact, the corner of her mouth was just beginning to twitch when the child threw a spanner into the machinery. She dropped her spoon, turned towards Kitty, smiled the biggest smile she could find, and said, 'Mama?'

'That does it,' Kitty declared grimly. She took off her enveloping napkin, wiped her chin, and made to get up.

'But you haven't finished your split,' Joel complained

'I've suddenly remembered an urgent errand. It's been a pleasure. I hope we'll meet again one day.' At which she climbed down from the stool, tried to take a couple of steps, felt the throbbing in her head, and fell backwards—into his arms. The dizzy spell passed quickly, but it was so comfortable there that she hated to move. Comfort, there's a word I haven't had the use of much lately, she told herself. Comfortable?

'We've got to stop meeting like this,' he whispered in her ear. 'The town is talking already!'

Kitty's face turned blush-red as she fumbled her way to her feet. 'Village,' she said authoritatively. 'It's a village, not a town. Northport is the town. This little place is known as the Head of the River. Excuse me, I *have* to go.'

'Of course you do,' he agreed. 'Go where?'

'Down on the Neck,' Kitty responded, referring to the little peninsula that stretched out into the ocean, known locally as Hopkins Neck.

'That's a long trip, Katherine.' She shivered at the use of her full name. He said it slowly, as if he were tasting, savouring it. And I'm next, she told herself, and I'd hate to be tasted by him! Wouldn't I?

'I have my ten-speed outside,' she told him. 'It won't take me long.'

'I have my van outside,' he countered. 'It'll be a lot less long. And I don't intend, after I've had the gall to almost knock your brains out, to let you go bicycling something over two miles in the hot sun!'

'I don't take orders,' she snapped at him. Meaning I don't take orders from strange men whom I've only known for a matter of hours and who have a very strange effect on my nerves, and who hope to palm a niece off on me for lord knows how long, and——

'And the van is air-conditioned,' he interrupted her thoughts.

'I'll take it, I'll take it,' Kitty said as she climbed back up on the stool. 'Let me just finish my banana split, will you?'

'Not exactly what I had in mind for a van,' said Kitty as she strolled across the village square to where Joel's vehicle was parked.

'So a mobile home,' Joel shrugged his shoulders as he unlocked the centre door. 'Sleeps four, seats eight, refrigerator, shower—we travel a lot, Mary and I do. That's to say, we formerly travelled a lot!'

Kitty slid gingerly into the front seat. The man was not one for taking hints. Probably the best approach would be with a baseball bat. 'That's not good for a baby,' she told him, preparing for lecture number 2A. 'I read somewhere that a child needs ties, a settled life.'

'See?' he chuckled as he climbed into the driver's seat. 'Just what I told you. Ties. Mary hates to be tied into that travel-seat!'

'Well, don't look at me,' Kitty snapped. 'I'm certainly not going to hold her all the way. You take a left here and go down the hill.'

'I know how to get to the Neck,' he reminded her. 'This happens to be my home town. So you don't believe in babies?'

Ah! At last he has the message, she thought. But don't overdo it. It might be fun to know this man—to a degree, that is. 'It isn't that I don't believe in babies,' she protested. 'For some I suppose it's a great idea. And some babies are cute. But they grow up, you know. What looks like a cute kid could grow up to be a juvenile delinquent. Have you ever thought of that?'

The air-conditioner was going at full speed, spreading welcome coolness. Kitty ran her hands up the back of her neck, pulled a pair of pins out of her bun, and let her long golden hair swing free. A moment's finger-combing undid the tight braids, and let it all hang out.

'Hey, look at you,' muttered Joel as they took the narrow curve on Thompson's Lane.

'I'd rather you looked at the road,' she replied. The Neck was very narrow at the point where the peninsula joined the mainland. So narrow and so low that at neap tides the connecting land was really a marsh, while at spring tides the peninsula often became an island. The

bridge that spanned the marsh had been called two lanes
wide, but truthfully it was only one and a half.

The peninsula rose abruptly above the marshes with
steep cliffs on the seaward side, and a gradual slope off
the other side, leading down on to the shore of Northport
River and Chamuchaset Bay. The road followed the in-
dentations about one third up that gradual slope, cutting
the peninsula into a shore-side and a cliff-side. The entire
area was caught in a tide of change; originally it had all
been working farms, now the developers were estab-
lishing tiny bedroom communities.

'All the way down to the end?' They had been driving
down the road for approximately twenty minutes.

'Almost,' she said. It was amazing how quiet it was
inside the van. In her own truck one had to yell to be
heard. She could almost hear her heart beat. 'There's
only one place farther out than I am. Those damn
Carmodys!'

'Ah, I thought I heard the name while we were in the
bank,' he said. 'Troublemakers, are they?'

'I don't really know,' Kitty confessed. 'The Carmodys
and the Andersons have been feuding for years. I don't
know when it started—probably in the 1900 era. But I've
been away for a long time. When I was a little girl nobody
lived up there in the big house. Since I've come back
there have been some comings and goings, but I've been
too busy to look into it. My brother would write from
time to time, and he didn't sound too cheerful about the
Carmodys. I'd rather not talk about them any more.
Here's my place. Turn right.'

The Anderson home was a combination of all the
possible architecture the founding United States could
provide. The centre core was a ramshackle clapboard
Cape Cod cottage. Two wings had been added at some
indeterminate time, almost matching the levels of the
cottage, but not quite. Out in the back were two old

barns, and one practically new portable aluminium building, sealed tight. Everything in sight was painted white—well, *had been* painted white. A great deal of the paint was peeling. A small garden set the house off from the road. Out at the back, acres of land were divided by log rick-rack fences, isolating fields of beautifully trimmed grass.

'And over there you see my neighbours,' Kitty grumbled. Joel turned to look down the hill. The entire area across the street was packed with tiny cottages, with streets leading down to the bay-beach. 'Used to be all trees, that area, and we kids could run down to the beach at any time, day or night. Now, if you don't belong to the community, you can't use the beach!'

'I suppose people *do* need houses,' he commented.

'That's not a low-cost housing development,' she muttered. 'You can't live in those band-boxes for less than two hundred thousand apiece! Every time I come out of my front door I have to close my eyes, so I don't throw up! And now they keep hounding me to sell the rest of the farm! Well, I'm darned if I will!' One of her tiny fists pounded into the other. 'You know what they told my brother? They were going to build a free summer camp for the poor kids from New Bedford and Fall River. Boy, they conned him to a fare-thee-well!'

'And I thought I heard something about a foreclosure?'

'Did you?' she asked bleakly. 'Not from me. But it's true. When my dad died Robert inherited all that land over there. He offered to sell about half of it to be used for the children's camp. He was using the rest of it for a new house he was building. Rob isn't a very—clever man. He's a farmer. So he gave the bank his power and asked them to conclude the deal for the camp. They did, and he never made a cent out of it. Then on top of all that they foreclosed on his mortgage loan because he

was short in one payment. Damn, if I could find out the
name of the people the bank sold that land to I'd raise
holy hell in this town! The Sheerin Corporation built the
houses, but that's always been a fly-by-night outfit.
Somebody bankrolled them from behind the scenes. I'd
love to know who that somebody was, but I can't get
the bank to tell me, and I wasn't here while the work
was going on. The people who live over there all think
I'm a plague-carrier, or I'm planning to dispossess them.
They won't tell me a thing. Well, one day I'll find out,
believe me!'

'Hey, I *am* sorry,' Joel answered. He was scanning the
area in a three-hundred-and-sixty-degree turn, one hand
held up to shade his eyes. Mary, clinging to his shoulder,
had been sleeping, and now she awoke and began to
whimper.

'Well, I'm the one who should be sorry,' Kitty told
him. 'Keeping you standing out here in the hot sun,
listening to my mad-list. The kid needs a change or
something. Come in and let me fix you a cup of coffee.'

Katherine Anderson was not house-proud. Only her
kitchen held that privilege. It had been modelled and
remodelled by dozens of Anderson women, trying to
impose *their* age on the age of the house, and not winning
too often. It was a big room. In the centre was a free-
standing table that served as counter and work space. A
large highly polished stove powered by bottled gas stood
against the north wall. The south wall was all windows,
bowed out into the sunshine, with an eating booth set
in the insert.

'I need the table,' said Joel as he stretched little Mary
out without waiting for Kitty's agreement. To her surprise he pulled all the necessaries out of the bag he carried
slung over one shoulder. It was not a routine Kitty knew

much about. She watched out of the corner of her eye as she heated water for instant coffee.

He was a different sort of man now, leaning over the child, tickling her, making faces, acting out some story that was all truth to both of them—and changing her nappy at the same time. The coffee was ready at the same time as the child. He gave the baby one more little tickle and set her down on the floor to run. She did, busily exploring her new little world. Good lord, Kitty thought. I haven't invited anyone into my home for years now, and here he is—with his niece running around my kitchen! Why? There was no answer, but a little tremor ran up her back. A pleasurable tremor such as she had not experienced before.

'You do that well,' she congratulated him, as she set out the coffee, and a plate of left-over cookies.

'Practice makes perfect,' said Joel with a perfectly straight face. 'Anyone can do it.'

'Not me,' she said glumly. 'I haven't a clue.'

'I'd be glad to teach you,' he assured her.

'No—no, I don't think I want to go that far. You'll make some woman a fine husband.' And I'll bet a girl would have to stand in line, or take a ticket, she whispered to herself. I wonder how it would be?

'Good coffee,' he said. 'If you can make coffee, you can change a baby.'

'Instant,' she reminded him, but she sipped her own with some pleasure.

'So's Mary,' he said. 'Instant, that is. No waiting.'

'I don't want to talk about babies,' Kitty replied. 'What do you do for a living, Mr—er—Joel? I take it you *are* employed?'

'Why, I believe so.' He pushed his chair back as Mary ran up to his knee, looked up at him appealingly, and used half her vocabulary. 'Nuncle Joe?' He picked her up and kissed her tiny nose. 'Yes, I'm employed,' he resumed. 'There's a family corporation, and I happen to have some sort of job within it.'

'I remember you said a large family,' she said. Her coffee mug was just cooling to the proper temperature. She surrounded it with both hands and took a sip.

'Did I? I don't remember. But yes, we have a big family. But the corporation is big enough to afford a job for all of us. Isn't that nice?'

'I wonder that the corporation wasn't able to provide a family that included a mother for Mary,' Kitty remarked.

'I didn't say we were a big *happy* family,' he added. 'Funny how busy some people get when there's a little girl to be taken care of. Originally, that is. Now, when it becomes apparent that little Mary has inherited both her father's and her mother's shares in the company, there's a lot of talk about rearranging things. Turning her over to some other couple in the family.'

Kitty took another sip from her mug. Black coffee. She hadn't even offered him milk and sugar! Her face turned red once again. Of all the things her mother had taught her, courtesy stood at the head of the list.

'I'm a terrible hostess,' she sighed. 'Would you like milk, sugar?'

'Skimmed milk?'

'I—I really don't know. I'll look. Are *you* dieting?'

'My family has a tendency to spread,' he replied solemnly. She looked him over carefully. He had not an ounce of excess flesh on his entire frame! Tendency, hah!

'Well, you'd notice if I were in my bathing suit,' he said. 'I'm a man who needs lots of outdoor exercise, and corporation-watching just doesn't hack it. Any skim milk?'

'As it happens I have a quart,' she said, taking a plastic container out and inspecting it suspiciously. 'But I'm never sure whether it's turned or not. Could you?'

'Nothing wrong with that,' he said, sniffing at the opened top. 'Now, an ounce or two, and—no, Mary, this isn't your kind. I have your cup in my pack.' He carried the child over to the table and fished out a small feeding container with a plastic non-spill lip. The little girl told him of her appreciation at great length. Kitty was unable to make out a single word.

'You communicate?' she queried.

'Of course. Didn't you hear?'

Kitty shook her head in disgust. 'I heard, but I didn't understand. You have to make some sort of language study?'

'You have to grow up with the child,' he chuckled, 'Now, tell me about all those threats, back at the bank?'

'I must have lost my temper,' she replied. 'I try not to do that. I've paid off all the loans outstanding on my property. And I've hired a lawyer. There's something fishy about this whole affair, and I intend to poke and pry——'

'Until something bites you?' he interjected.

'Until *someone* tries to bite me. There's a difference.'

'I can see that, Katherine Anderson. And now I've got to get home—I have some appointments this afternoon. Say goodbye, Mary.'

'G'bye,' the child said. 'Kiss?'

Kitty bent down awkwardly and exchanged a wet salute. It was not quite her thing, but she knew better than to wipe her mouth while the pair of them were watching.

'And now me,' the big husky red-head said.

'Hey——' Kitty started to say. There wasn't room for the rest of the protest. His kiss was moist, but not wet, warm, but not overheated. He sealed her up within herself for just a fraction of a second. Like that of an automobile which had lost its radiator, her temperature went up like a shot, chills ran up her spine, and she was totally at a loss when he finally set her aside.

'Very nice,' he said. It was too much for Kitty.

'Very nice?' she snapped at him. 'You've got a nerve, Joel—whatever your name is! I don't go around letting strange men kiss me!' With a blatant gesture she scrubbed at her lips.

'Mama,' the little girl said.

'Now we *have* to go home,' said Joel.

'I hope it's a long way off, and I've put you considerably out of your way,' Kitty snapped, her eyes shooting laser death-rays at him.

'As it happens, it's not out of my way at all,' he replied. 'Just up the hill, for a fact, although I guess I'll have to go back a mile or two and go round the hill.'

'You——' she spluttered. 'You live up there in the big house?'

'I believe I do,' he said quietly. 'It's been fun, Katherine. We'll come by again tomorrow and see how you're doing.'

'Darned if you will,' she told him. 'Just what is your name?'

'Joel,' he said patiently, as if drilling a subnormal student. 'Joel.'

'The rest of your name,' she insisted. 'Your family name!'

'Oh, that? Carmody. Joel Michael Carmody. And if there's anything else you want to know, I'll tell you about it tomorrow.'

'The devil you will!' she snarled at him. 'Get out of my house! Carmody! I'll have to fumigate the place!'

'And we enjoyed meeting you too.' He chucked her under her chin, the baby's soft warm hands caressed her face, and they tramped out and were gone.

For a moment Kitty stood beside her serving counter, one hand on its solid surface, bracing her shivering self.

Carmody! The arch-villain himself. And I—lord, I *liked* him! she thought. It was too much for an ordinary mind to comprehend. Wearily she went out into the living-room and plumped herself down on the couch for a long think.

CHAPTER TWO

THE little brook was hardly big enough to deserve the name. It originated in a spring near the top of the ridge, then sidled and crabbed and sparkled down to almost the length of the peninsula, where it dived off into the Northport River. Occasionally it stopped on the way, held up in its passage by granite outcroppings, until it formed a pool and then fell over the edge, creating a tiny waterfall. Trees guarded the brook's passage, old willows which had stood sentry since the Wampanoag Indians had been driven out of the area.

Kitty stood on the little knoll on the north side of the brook and used her binoculars to study the fields in front of her. It was a detailed study, and doing it correctly meant the difference between putting steak on her table or opening another can of soup. She was just entering some figures into her notebook when the voice sounded at her elbow. 'Watching the grass grow?'

She put her pencil down slowly, using the time to count up to ten—and back downwards again—before she looked up. 'It *had* to be you,' she snapped. 'Yes, that's exactly what I'm doing.' Some time during the night she had reasoned out her concerns about this man. He had some strange attraction for her, but his name was Carmody. Her brother didn't like the Carmodys. She had never been quite clear what had caused the friction between Robert and the Carmodys, but her brother's word was enough, wasn't it?

And this morning, when she stepped out into the furnace heat of August, there were all those cottages across the street, forty-six of them, crowded together on land only capable of supporting twenty! Just the sight of them was enough to fire her anger. Could it be that a Carmody was responsible?

'In case you don't know it, Mr Carmody, the property line between our farms is that little brook. The *other* side of that brook, to be specific.'

'Why, that's wonderful,' he crowed. 'You don't change a whit, do you? You're every bit as mean in the morning as you are in the afternoon!'

'Every bit,' she assured him. 'Now, if you've something important to do, you won't let me keep you, will you?'

'Nicely put, Kitty. I——'

'Miss Anderson, please.'

'Say, I was wrong, wasn't I?' He was wearing a decrepit ten-gallon cowboy hat. He took it off and wiped his brow on the sleeve of his shirt. Kitty was too curious not to bite.

'You were wrong?'

'Of course. You're meaner in the morning than you are in the afternoon.'

'And you're as big a bore at any time of day,' she snapped. 'My brother wrote me a great deal about you Carmodys. Why don't you go away?'

He leaned back against the bole of one of the willow trees. 'How can that be?' he mused. 'I never met your brother, and I haven't been inside the state of Massachusetts in years. Not counting the last three days, of course.'

'Of course,' she muttered sarcastically. And if he isn't lying? 'Look, I'm working. Goodbye.'

'Working? I don't see anything happen. Let me watch. I need a job like yours.'

'You should be so lucky,' she was about to tell him, when she sensed trouble. Up the hill, perhaps a hundred yards away, a group of some six or seven horses had come over the brook and through the trees, and was racing up and down in her precious meadow! 'Hell and damnation!' she yelled as she ran for the barn. It was a long run, even though downhill. She was almost out of breath when she climbed aboard her multi-wheeled tractor, kicked the diesel engine into action, and roared out on to the narrow path that led towards the invaders. As she passed Joel Carmody he was waving that hat of his, and shouting something at her, to which she paid as much attention as it was worth.

The horses watched as the tractor entered the field with them. A couple had dropped off and were munching at her precious grass. The other five took the tractor as a challenge, and charged down at her, circled around, and came back again.

'Get out of here, you monsters!' she yelled at the top of her voice. The horses paid her no attention at all. Her trained hand moved to the mixture control on the engine, jogged it a couple of times, and waited until the diesel backfired with a rattle and a terrible smell. All the horses began to pay her some attention at that. She advanced the throttle and the little six-wheeled tractor bounced across the meadow in their direction.

The leader of the group, an over-aged stallion, brought his little herd into some semblance of order and urged them up the hill. Kitty, not accustomed to herding freethinkers, brought the tractor to a halt until she was sure which way they were about to run, then she slapped the throttle again and pushed them smartly across the boundary brook. She might have gone across herself, but by that time Joel Carmody had caught up with her, climbed up on the rumbling tractor, and clamped a hand on top of her throttle fingers.

'Just what the hell are you doing?' he roared at her.

'What do you *think* I'm doing?' she muttered as the engine slowed and grew silent.

'Idiot! Don't you know that those five mares might all be in foal?'

'I don't care if they're in Connecticut,' she returned. 'They have no business coming across my boundaries and ruining my grass! Let me go!'

He did, but outside the glassed-in cab of the machine, and with a thump that shook her knees as her feet hit the ground.

'Look,' he snapped, 'if any one of those mares miscarries I'm going to sue the pants off you!'

'I'll bet you'd like that,' she said. 'A typical reaction of a chauvinist male—Carmody!'

His frown faded away, and was replaced by a grin as he looked her over. 'Maybe I would at that,' he chuckled. 'Now, would you kindly tell me what that was all about? Those are very expensive thoroughbreds, every one of them.'

'And that's very expensive grass,' Kitty informed him.

'I wish I understood. You're raising a golf course or something?'

'I'm raising grass,' she insisted. 'The very best grass in the world. If this were a field of corn would you let your darn horses run through it?'

'Of course not. But that's only——'

'Grass?' she interrupted.

'Maybe you'd better explain.'

I don't know why I should, she told herself. Look at the silly ape, standing there grinning at me. You'd think he hadn't had breakfast, and I was about to be the first course. I liked him better when he had the baby in hand! Yes, her conscience teased. You liked him very much, didn't you, Katherine? 'Oh, shut up,' Kitty muttered.

'I know you don't like people,' Joel continued, 'but does that apply to horses too?'

It was one of the great miseries of her life, to have a patrician nose down which to stare, but not being able to find anyone short enough to use it on. As now. He would not have been noticeable among the players of the Boston Celtics basketball team, but sharing a meadow with Kitty Anderson, he was a sure winner. If you don't tell him something, she concluded to herself, he's just going to stand there and stare—or perhaps think up something worse to say or do.

'Listen very carefully, Mr Carmody,' she said. 'Read my lips. This is a farm. I grow grass. When people want to buy grass I sell it, in rolls that are two feet wide and ten feet long. I make money from this, which I use to buy food and drink. Most of my customers are developers. Would you believe, I even sold grass to those—people across the street! Which shows you how much pride *I've* got. Now, since I've not had horse troubles before, and you are recently arrived, I suppose them to be *your* horses?'

'As it happens,' he drawled, 'you're right, ma'am. Can't say that I ever had this kind of trouble back in Kentucky.'

'Perhaps this New England venture was just not meant to be,' she suggested drily. 'Why don't you just pack up and go back to—Kentucky? Or Texas. I hear they're mighty fond of horses in Texas.'

'Y'know, a fellow could get the feeling he wasn't welcome,' mused Joel as he put his hat carefully back on his head. 'Lucky I'm not sensitive. You want to be careful with your face, ma'am.'

'My face?' She had done it again without thinking.

'Yes, ma'am. I can see there's a smile trying to get through. If it does it'll crack the whole affair up, and leave you nothing but the uglies!'

Kitty could feel the anger boil. If she spat, she knew that the ground under her feet would steam. *Uglies*, indeed! There had been a time, and not too long ago, either, when she had been the belle of more than one ball. *Uglies*, indeed! But somehow her facile tongue had got itself twisted up into a knot.

'Could you just—go, Mr Carmody?'

'Joel, not Mr Carmody. He was my father.'

'Just—dammit!' One tear slid down from under her right eyelid and coursed down her cheek, brushing the perspiration aside.

'Hey, I didn't mean—yes, ma'am, I'm going. And I'll have this section fenced before we turn the horses loose again.' He tipped his hat, looked at her anxiously, and turned to walk up the hill. Kitty watched.

There was something about his solidly dependable— good lord, where had *that* word come from?—something about his solid figure that bespoke confidence, assurance. He was the sort of man a girl might possibly count on. Which, she knew, was sheer nonsense. There wasn't *any* man a girl could count on for anything! And you mustn't let him get away unscathed, she told herself.

'Hey!' she called after him. Joel stopped, almost straddling the brook.

'When you come next time, bring a shovel. Your damn horses left me something more than good intentions!' He grinned at her and waved his hat. She watched as he strode up the hill, his shoulders back, head up, moving with the easy grace of an athlete. The sort of man who fulfilled her adolescent dreams. The thought stirred her into nervousness. 'I'm not ready for that,' she muttered. You are too! her conscience roared back. More than ready! 'So maybe I am,' she retorted to the listening world, 'but——' Can't think of an excuse? her inner guide asked sarcastically. 'Oh, shut up,' Kitty growled as she shrugged her shoulders and turned back to the tractor, meaning to have the last word, even with herself.

But that little internal voice jumped ahead of her again. Now if only he weren't a Carmody, it reminded her.

She knuckled the tear out of her eye as she swung back up into the cab.

Kitty spent an hour overhauling the tractor. She had collected enough orders to put a major cutting in hand. The cutter-sled, glistening in oil and attention, stood in one corner of the aluminium barn. The parts of the tractor were scattered over the remaining area. She knew all the individual parts, and could put the machine back together again blindfolded. She was up to her elbows in grease when her lawyer walked in.

'Hey, I couldn't find anyone at the house,' Faith Latimore said. Kitty waved a welcoming greasy hand, warning against coming closer. Faith was all blonde beauty, dimity and femininity, a disguise which hid her very hard heart, and her expertise at law. In fact, it was said around the court-houses in Bristol County that Faith was the second-best female lawyer in the state.

'I don't know how you do all this,' said Faith, looking around. 'I even have to get my brother to help fix my bicycle! What's all this I hear about you and a certain good-looking man?'

'Nothing!' Kitty was so aggravated that she almost shouted. 'I don't want to hear another word about— well, it's not true, whatever you heard. And besides that, he's not all that good-looking!'

'No, of course not,' Faith replied, cocking one eyebrow up in absolute disbelief. 'But then you know all about men, don't you?' It came out as a positive statement which they both knew was a terrible lie, but Kitty was not about to let the notion stand unsupported.

'It all comes from a tour in the Air Force,' she explained, regaining her composure. 'They teach you everything you want to know about men and machines. And some things you don't want to know!'

Faith nodded sagely, as if she believed every bit of it. 'And then you went to computer school?'

'Why not? A girl has to make a living. Look at you, graduating from Harvard Law?'

'Let me tell you something you obviously don't know,' said Faith. 'The hardest exam given at Harvard is the entrance exam. I take it you're going to cut some more grass?'

'Tomorrow,' Kitty sighed. 'I don't look forward to it, but——'

'Did you pay off the loan?'

'Every darn cent. As far as I know, I'm free and clear from the bank!'

'Good. Then I guess we can get started, huh?'

'Faith, I'm not sure—this law business is all strange to me. Tell me again what we're up to.'

'We're going on a fishing expedition. You think there was some hanky-panky that went on with this development across the street. An earlier restraint on the usage, a curious result with percolation tests, an unusual financing? So OK. Somewhere in the town's system of paperwork there's bound to be some little something that can tell us what we want to know. The Freedom of Information Act is a law that requires government agencies to divulge all those interesting things which they'd rather not reveal. So we go into court tomorrow, and file for release of all perk tests in connection with this development.'

'But maybe we won't find anything.'

'Maybe we won't. But we'll stir up a fuss, and then we'll file for any other information we can think of. And we'll keep it up until something gives. OK?'

'OK, OK. What do *I* do?'

'Keep your head down, wash your hands, and sign here!'

By two o'clock that afternoon Kitty had reassembled the tractor, fired it up for a test run, and gone into the house to shower and change. A quick look in the full-length bathroom mirror confirmed what she had been afraid of.

Her nose was sunburned to a fare-thee-well, the line of freckles across her shoulders had grown deeper, and her glossy blonde hair needed considerable attention. Hands on hips, she swivelled to one side. Her shoulders were not bad at all, her hips curved as well as any girl might require. Legs, long for her body size, but well shaped, and perhaps her breasts weren't all that small after all?

'Wishful thinking,' she told herself derisively as she reached for a pullover shirt, a pair of cotton briefs, and a pair of shorts. 'And tell me why, Katherine, does this subject come up all of a sudden?' It was a question she didn't want to answer. In fact she didn't want to find out the veriest part of the answer. Joel Carmody's face kept haunting her!

She was looking around the bathroom, undecided about cleaning it up, when the hail came from the front door. A man. And not a doubt about *which* man, she told herself as she padded barefooted towards the door. He was already inside.

'Well, I thought maybe you didn't hear me,' he explained.

'That's a poor excuse.' But for some reason Kitty was unable to work up a real head of steam at him. Perhaps it was because Faith had signalled the second phase of the Anderson attack. Or perhaps it was because the temperature outside had dropped all the way down to eighty-five degrees. Or perhaps it had something to do with the lop-sided smile he gave her. It had a sort of boyish look to it, a Peter Pan look.

'I'm very busy,' she told him.

'You surely don't look it, ma'am.'

'Don't give me that ma'am business, and get your shoe out of my door. I'm very busy. Today is a farm workday.' A brief pause to scan his face. He wasn't overly impressed so far. 'And I have a hundred things to do.'

His face brightened. 'Me too—a hundred and ten, probably.'

Kitty sighed. 'I'm glad we've agreed on something. Goodbye, Mr Carmody.'

He took a couple of steps towards the door and grinned down at her. 'Mary's spent the whole morning talking about you. Chatter, chatter, chatter! That kid is mad about you, Kitty Anderson. And I have to go to Taunton for a meeting of the board of the Jimmy Fund.'

'That's the Children's Cancer Fund?' He nodded.

An uneasy feeling ran up Kitty's spine. There was more here than met the eye. Any time soon he would say 'Hey presto!' and produce something that looked magical and tasted foul. What could the man be up to? Nevertheless, even a grouch was entitled to feel good when nice things were said.

'I appreciate that your niece likes me,' she murmured. 'Not that I said or did anything to make her feel so.'

Joel shrugged his shoulders at her. 'Fishing for compliments? You don't have to. You started all the fun in the bank. I'll tell you something, her poor dumb uncle would never have thought of a thousand paper aeroplanes floating around the bank!'

'More than a thousand,' she corrected stiffly. 'Goodbye?'

'That child would just love to spend a little time with you.' This was spoken in a hearty avuncular tone, and Kitty was caught unawares.

Without thinking, she took a step or two towards the door, trying to shepherd him out. 'That *would* be nice.' His face lit up like a neon bar sign on a Saturday night, and Kitty knew she had put her foot in it!

'I knew you'd feel that way!' His little grin grew to massive size as he stepped outside, still holding the door open. 'And certainly there's no time like the present!' One big arm disappeared from sight and then came back, clutching little Mary by the bright red braces that held up her minuscule shorts.

He set the little girl down on her pudgy feet. 'There now, pet, didn't I tell you it would work out all right?' One little nudge sent the child wobbling across the room towards Kitty.

'Hey, just a minute!' she protested.

'Mama!' the little girl squealed as she plumped down in the middle of the floor.

'Everything you need is in this bag. I'll be back for her at four o'clock.' The bag smacked on to the linoleum. The child squealed again as she cantilevered herself back up to her feet. The door slammed.

'Hey, wait a darn minute!' roared Kitty as she raced across the floor. That man was already climbing into the battered old Jeep parked in her drive. She went out on to the front stoop, a large chunk of bare slate. The minute the soles of her bare feet hit the sun-warmed stone she knew she had made another mistake. She yelped and did a little Indian dance.

'You can't do this!' she bellowed after him. Joel waved, smiled, and went bouncing off down to the road. 'You can't do this to me!' she roared again, but he was already out of sound range.

Miserable   rotten   chauvinistic—Carmody! Kitty thought. Her little clenched fists beat against the air. The screen door creaked behind her and she turned around. 'Mama,' the little child said. 'Nuncle Joe go?'

Kitty swallowed twice, hard. It wasn't the kid's fault that her Nuncle was a very large pain in the neck.

One more deep rattling sigh shook Kitty's small frame. 'Yes, your nuncle is gone—dammit, your *uncle*! Now what do we do, kid?'

One of the major problems that rose out of having declared war on an entire village was that there weren't many people willing to lend a hand—or an ear, in this case. After having made six telephone calls without success, Kitty finally gave it up and called the emergency room at St Luke's Hospital.

'Yes,' the nurse repeated for the third time, 'we handle emergency work of all kinds. Just what seems to be wrong with the child?'

'She won't eat,' Kitty snapped. 'I told you that the first time.'

'Well, it's a hot day, Mrs——?'

'Miss. I told you that too. *Miss* Anderson. *Miss*! Look, I'm on a farm outside of Northport, and there's nobody else here but me. The kid is maybe two or three years old, and she won't eat.'

'And does she seem to have any pain?'

'No. She's laughing at me, dammit. She just won't eat!'

'Don't get excited, Miss Anderson.' Nurse Millie Bates had accumulated a very large bag of experience with unmarried mothers. 'If the child isn't hungry, she won't eat. Do you have a formula for her?'

'A what? The kid didn't come with any instructions, lady. No formula. All she has is one more set of diapers and this milk-bottle with the nozzle on it. But she won't touch that either.'

'It's hard to offer advice at this distance,' Nurse Bates answered. 'What is it that you're trying to feed her?'

'Chop suey. It's hot and they deliver, you know.'

Millie Bates put her hand over the mouthpiece of the telephone and said, 'Oh, lord, another one of those!' Dr Smithson, who was leaning over her desk looking for a particular piece of paper, chuckled.

'She has a cute little girl baby, and she doesn't know how to operate it,' the nurse repeated.

'Let me help,' the doctor offered as he picked up the telephone. 'Miss? The child needs something simple and bland. Something soft. Apple sauce? No, baked beans aren't particularly good. Oh? She likes them? Well——' and here the doctor called on his thirty years of experience '—if she'll eat them, let her. Yes, they all spit food out. Miss? We're pretty busy here. Give it a try, and—yes, we're just like the military. Put on a Bandaid and, if it hasn't stopped bleeding, call me tomorrow. Yes. And the same to you!' He slammed the telephone down.

'Woman hasn't the brains to *have* a child. Ought to be a law!'

While at the other end Kitty slammed her telephone back down in its cradle and faced the uncommonly patient little girl across from her. 'You'd think they'd know, being an emergency ward,' she mourned.

'Nuncle Joe,' the child told her as she managed to get the bean plate between both her chubby little hands, then gleefully tipped it over and on to the floor.

'Nuncle Joe I'm going to kill!' Kitty snarled, and the baby's lower lip began to tremble. 'Only joking, kid. Honest.' She swept the little girl up out of the improvised high-chair, disregarding the array of food decorating the improvised bib. 'Hey now, no crying! That's not allowed.' Vague in Kitty's memories was a mother who had walked her up and down the floor, patting her on the back. Why not?

Six steps did the work. Little Mary babbled for a moment, then rested her head on Kitty's shoulder, snorted a couple of times, and promptly went to sleep. Kitty took one more trip across the room before she stopped, but halting was not to be allowed. The child struggled to force her eyes open, and began to cry. The pacing resumed.

The warm little head resting in the junction between her neck and shoulder gave Kitty pause to think. She had never been family-orientated. No babies and husbands and slippers by the fire had ever entered into her life-plans. Yes, the baby was cute; yes, the uncle was— wow! But lord, I'm too scared to get down on the floor and wrestle with him, she told herself firmly. I'm better off with my software and flow-charts! Aren't I?

At every turn, at the door, Kitty managed to stare out at the north paddock, the place where she should already have half the sod cut. The wind was ruffling the grass out there. Nothing else was happening. The leased trucks would be at her door in the morning. The sod had to be cut by then, and rushed through half of New England. Seventy-two hours after cutting the shipments would be worthless! And here she was, tied down by one homely little kid and her despicable nuncle—uncle. There was really only one answer to her problem.

The kid lived but half a mile away, all uphill, of course. There must be someone in the oversized mansion who knew what to do about the—child. And stop calling her a kid, Kitty lectured herself. If she's only going to be quiet while you're walking her, why not walk her up the hill and give her back to her family?

It took her a few minutes to find her shoes and stuff her feet into them, without putting the baby down. Another minute or two was sacrificed to a hat-search. The kid—the child—had thin silky hair and a light complexion. She would surely burn.

Kitty's own straw hat, wide-brimmed and ancient, was the cure. Wearing it on her own head, with the baby on her shoulder, would ensure that both would have some protection. Another sigh shook her as she rearranged her load. It was hard for her to face the fact that she knew so little about children. But Kitty's mother had died before her only daughter was six months old. Her father had raised her like another boy—a match for her brother. It had all been fun, that growing up, with no thought to the nurturing needs that any little girl might have learned. Any American kid could learn to open a can or heat a TV dinner, and what else would she need? But now that she knew she had missed something, for some perverse reason Kitty assigned the blame for all that to—who else?—Carmody!

The first part of the hike was easy. The slope of the ridge was not great until one crossed over the brook. They stopped for a moment at the pool just behind the house. It was cool under the trees—or perhaps it was the babble of the brook that made it seem so. The child awoke and was enthralled by the movement of the water. Kitty lowered her until her feet were bathed, and little Mary squealed in delight. Not thinking, Kitty lowered her further, until her tiny feet grounded on the sandy bottom. Fifteen minutes later, with both of them soaked, the parade up the hill began again.

What did you do to entertain a child in your arms? Your aching arms? You sang little songs, part of which you remembered from your own girlhood—and filled in the remainder with nonsense words. None of which detracted from Mary's enjoyment. Then you picked a buttercup and held it to the child's nose while she mashed the petals up into butter. And when you reached the fence that surrounded the big house, you jiggled the child in rhythm as you tried to explain to the two nosey mastiffs who interrupted your parade that you have not come to burn the house down.

It was the child again who saved the world. She wriggled in Kitty's arms, reaching down with both hands, the fingers clutching and unclutching as if she were waving. 'G'bye, doggie,' the child laughed.

Both the animals, either entranced or accustomed to the play, gave a little bark and fell behind the procession. And so they went around the big two-storey house, whose white paint flashed almost painfully in the reflected sunlight, and whose highly polished windows glittered sarcastically at them.

'And who would let us in?' Kitty murmured. Mary gabbled something incomprehensible. 'Very well said,' Kitty told her. She was beginning to feel a certain small affection for the little tyke. There was a very large brass knocker on the door, a shaped lion's head at the end of a metallic circle. She shifted the child to the other arm. Her right hand and her shoulder were beginning to ache, but the hand was strong enough to give the knocker an enthusiastic bang. The child, naturally, wanted to do it for herself. Kitty leaned forward so that the little hand could reach, but before the child could try it out the door was snatched away from in front of her.

The man was about medium height, carefully dressed in well-pressed dark trousers, a shirt, and a waistcoat. The blast of cold air that clung to him spoke of airconditioning. The frowning face indicated a desire to close the door and get back into the cold air. 'Madam?' he queried.

'Look, I live down the hill, and——'

'Do you really?' he interrupted. 'Mrs Carmody is busy at the moment, perhaps you could come another day.'

It was all just too much. The sun was high, and Kitty's temper was higher. Her shirt clung to her like a second skin, sweat-soaked. Her arm, which had borne the weight of the baby all that distance, felt as if it were about to break. And now this!

She stuck the toe of her shoe into the open door and glared at the man. 'How would you like,' she asked sweetly, 'a punch in the mouth?'

'Well, really!' he gasped. It seemed to be his favourite word. But as Kitty forced herself by him into the cool hall he backed out of the way.

'You said Mrs Carmody?' she asked. 'And who are you?'

'I'm Carswell, the butler,' the man replied.

'You recognise this child, Carswell? Do you?'

'I—er—yes, madam. She looks vaguely familiar.'

Vaguely familiar? Kitty looked down at the child in alarm. Perhaps the chocolate ice-cream had been a mistake. The kid had eaten it with enthusiasm, and half her face was brown. There seemed to be another mixture or two to go with the ice-cream. That dark dribble off Mary's mouth might easily be soy sauce; the yellow was the failed experiment with egg salad. And you've got the same mixture all over your blouse, she noted as she looked down.

'All she needs is a little wash,' she explained. 'Why don't you take it—her—to wherever you do that sort of thing and get her cleaned up? She'll be as good as new then.' She leaned in the butler's direction, meaning to make the transfer.

'Oh, no, madam,' he responded, backing away. 'Children are not in my line of work, you understand. The last time I—they asked me to hold the child she bit me.'

'Well, she's not in my line of work either,' Kitty replied. 'Where's this crazy uncle of hers?'

'Uncle? Oh, you mean Mr Joel? He's not at home at the moment. Why don't you go away and try again later?'

Kitty shook her head in disgust, and looked around. The door to the adjacent room stood open. Inside she could see at least one chair. All I need, she told herself as she strengthened her grip on Mary and brushed by the butler.

'Carswell,' she announced in her best movie imitation of a *grande dame,* 'you may tell somebody that I'm here with Mary.'

'May I ask who you are?'

'Who I am? Who? Katherine Anderson, that's who I am.'

'Do we know you?' asked the butler.

'*We* do now. Just go and announce me—or whatever it is you do. And bring me a wet face-cloth. Jump!' That last word was a wild inclination to make the house tremble. It had no effect on the house, but Carswell was completely taken in by it all, and disappeared. 'Oh, really!' Kitty mocked as he scrambled around the corner of the door.

Mary evidently was a stranger to the room they were in. The walls were panelled, with a deep beige rug, and the chairs were built for people twice Kitty's size. She sank back in one of them and was immediately bothered because her feet failed to reach the floor. Mary wriggled out of her arms, slid down her length, and plopped down on to the rug. The child was struggling between happiness and discomfort. A little puddle of water was gathering on the carpet under her feet. And an irate woman steamed in through the door.

'Just what is going on here?' the newcomer demanded. She must have seen a great many movies too, Kitty told herself. Do I stand up and bow? Or shall I just sit here and tremble? The latter, of course. Her military training had taught her that cowering was sometimes the safer alternative.

'You! Who are you?'

'Just a neighbour,' Kitty said. And then for a little embellishment, 'I found this kid down by the brook. I think she's one of yours.'

'You found——?'

'Down by the brook,' Kitty repeated, nodding sagely. 'Your husband left the kid there.' And if that doesn't burn the soles of his feet, nothing will, she thought.

'But she's——'

'Dirty, yes. She wouldn't eat the regular dinner, so I called a doctor about it, and ended up feeding her ice-cream. She prefers chocolate to vanilla. But of course you know that, being her mother and all.' And what a lucky woman you are, married to Joel, having this lovely child. For a moment Kitty hid her eyes and blinked. I should be so lucky!

'I am *not* that child's mother!' snapped the woman.

'Ah. Well, I didn't think you'd find it insulting. Stepmother. How's that?'

'And not her stepmother either. How dare you?'

'Yes, well, I guess I've mixed it all up.' Kitty sighed and shook her head at her own stupidity. As lovely as Mrs Carmody is, she doesn't have any of the things that I'd be jealous about, does she? So I might as well plough madly ahead! 'And since I can't get any worse off, and you've got such a nice red rug, I think the child needs a dry diaper!'

'Oh, my lord,' Mrs Carmody groaned. 'I told John I'd have nothing to do with the child, but he insisted that he *had* to have the little monster live here just because his brother said so. Spineless, the whole lot of them. Joel's been away for years; he comes home and roars at us all, and right away everyone is——'

'Excuse me,' Kitty interrupted. 'I'm a little mixed up. John? And Joel? I know Joel has just come up from Kentucky, but do you mean he hasn't been around here in the last five years or so?'

'In the last seven years!' the woman exclaimed as she reached into a jewel-studded case on the table and helped herself to a cigarette. 'Like the seven-year-itch, that man. *John* is my husband.'

'He *does* get under your skin very easily, doesn't he?' Kitty mused. But her mind was running madly uphill. If it were true that Joel Carmody hadn't been around for so many years, then Kitty's brother must have been referring to some other Carmody. The John whom this woman had just mentioned? Strange, how comforting the idea was. How heart-warming!

And at that moment the front door banged open, and a clatter of claws indicated that the mastiffs had come inside. Come inside, and were hunting. Kitty drew her legs up into her chair as if that might be some protection. Mrs Carmody gave a little scream and backed away towards the windows. Little Mary wobbled on unsteady legs towards the huge beasts, a big smile on her face as she gabbled at high speed.

Joel Carmody, standing indolently against the door jamb, said, 'Well, how cosy! What, do we suppose, is going on here?'

CHAPTER THREE

'I *DID* begin to worry when I found neither of you at home,' Joel Carmody said. His little niece shouted in glee, brushed by the dogs, and wobbled in his direction. His outstretched hands snatched her up, pressed her against his cotton shirt, and his smile faded gradually away as his hand came away from her bottom, wet.

'You didn't change her, Kitty?'

'Change her? No, why should I?' Kitty moved back from him, back into a window corner. This man was just too dangerous for words. 'You had no right foisting that kid off on me,' she said crossly.

'But you didn't change her? Why?'

'Stop nagging at me! No, I didn't change her. Just what in the world are you up to? Why should I be the one elected to do all your dirty work?'

'But the child is soaking wet, all the way up to her shoulders, Kitty!'

'Miss Anderson, if you please. If you feel all that badly about it, why the devil don't you train the kid?'

'I was about to start this summer,' he replied. There was an apology in his voice. 'But unfortunately we had to move. You can't train a child in unsettled conditions.'

And how in the world was I supposed to know that? Kitty thought. He was unloading a guilt-trip on her shoulders, and she hardly knew what to say next. 'We—er—we fell into the brook. We were—doing something or other, and I was holding her, and—we fell. And you can wipe that supercilious grin off your face, Mr Know-it-all Carmody! Just because I don't know——' and her

46

anger reached such a height that the words leaked out '—I don't know *how* to change her!'

Joel looked unbelieving for a moment, then broke out into a roar of laughter as he fell back into one of the overstuffed chairs. 'I don't believe it,' he said, wiping tears from his eyes. Little Mary, riding his shoulder, was entranced by the laughter and added a giggle or two of her own.

'I suppose you think that's funny!' Kitty snarled at the pair of them.

'Obviously.' He managed to get his eyes clear. '*Any* woman knows how to change a baby!'

'Is that darn so?' muttered Kitty. She snatched the child out of his arms and turned to Mrs Carmody. 'Here, you change the kid. Every woman knows how!' The woman stared at her, her brown eyes expanding, almost as if she disbelieved what was going on.

'What's your name?' she mumbled. 'Anderson?'

'Yes, Anderson. Change the kid's diapers.'

'Who, me? Not a chance.' The woman held up two hands as if to protect herself, sidled by the pair of them, and ran for the door.

'See!' Kitty exclaimed. 'Even your own wife doesn't know how to do it!'

'Spare me that burden,' he said as he dug into his pocket for a handkerchief. 'Jessica happens to be my *brother's* wife, not mine.' He used the handkerchief to wipe his own brow, then reached out to do the same for the baby.

'Nuncle Joe?' the child managed, leaning in his direction with both arms wide. The transfer was made.

'I just don't believe it,' he repeated as he dabbed at the wet little face.

'Believe it,' Kitty insisted. 'Would you expect a boy to be able to change a diaper?'

'Some could.' He nodded. 'Not many, unless they had younger siblings.'

'Well, then, I was raised as a boy,' said Kitty. 'And was the baby of the family. Do you know the proper tension to apply to bolts in a J52 jet engine?'

'Me? Of course not.'

'Well, I do. So why should it be so terrible that I don't know how to change a diaper? How old-fashioned do you have to get? Do you think women are born with all that stuff in their genes?'

'You're a strange girl, Kit.' He shook his head again. 'Well, the only answer is that I'll have to teach you, right?'

'Wrong, Mr Carmody. Look at me. I'm wet and I'm tired and I'm several hours behind in my work. My leased trucks will be at my door at eight o'clock tomorrow morning, and, because of your arrant stupidity, I won't be ready. I don't have the time to learn to change diapers. And I don't know that I have the inclination. I suppose you and your brother——'

'John,' he inserted. 'My brother John. His wife Jessica.'

'Yes, well, I suppose between you all you can get the kid—the child taken care of. Now, if you should ever feel you have a need for my help in the same circumstances, Mr Carmody, *forget it*!' and with that roar of anguish she brushed by him and made for the front door.

Carswell the butler got there before her, politely opening the door for her, and closing it—perhaps a little too enthusiastically—after she had gone out. Kitty paused for a second on the front stoop. 'And the same to you, butler,' she muttered. She stalked down the hill, but every step brought new emotions, took her further away from Joel, further away from the mystery that she *had* to solve. 'There's no amount of anger that you can muster that will blot him out,' she told herself. 'Darn fool! What a stupid mess to get yourself into!'

Inside the house Joel Carmody stretched his little niece out on her back on the thick pile rug, and stripped her. 'Get her bag, Carswell,' he ordered. 'The lady must have brought it up with her?'

'Yes, sir.' The butler managed to locate the tote bag out by the front door, and brought it back, holding it carefully between two fingers as if it were germ-ridden. This was *certainly* not the type of house he wanted to work in, he told himself as he watched the chairman of the board of a multi-billion-dollar enterprise kneel down on the floor to dry and powder and put a nappy on young Miss Mary.

Kitty was back home in twenty minutes. It wasn't a long trip, all downhill, but she was tired and puzzled and having a little trouble breathing. She had more than one reason for hating the Carmodys, after what her brother had written to her, and now this insufferable day's worth of Joel Carmody! So why should she be so disturbed by her own bad manners? Joel's face kept popping up in front of her, and could be blamed once again when a tear blinded Kitty so that she stumbled into the brook and slid down into the pool! Spluttering, she clawed her way out, resolving to pay more attention to her hatreds and less to her dreams.

A hot shower did something for her. Hot water to soak in, a warm meal to follow, and dry clothes. Working clothes. The warm meal consisted of a TV dinner, chicken parts and mashed potatoes, warmed in the gas stove. As she prepared it she glared out of the side windows at the subdivision across the street. Electric lights gleamed over there. And as soon as I get the money, I'm going to splurge on electricity, she assured herself. But she knew it was a dream.

She was back in the barn by seven-thirty. The cutting sled was ready, its blade honed to a knife-edge. She expertly backed her tractor up into the towing bight, fastened the locks and safety shields, and drove the whole apparatus out into the twilight. There were spotlights on top of the diesel cab. She turned them on and watched as the sled followed her out. Everything seemed to be working right.

A sod-cutting tow had to be handled with extreme care. Maximum speed on the road, with the blade up, was five miles an hour. It took fifteen minutes to juggle the entire apparatus up into the far corner of the meadow. There had to be a strip of grass on either side of the sled, room for the tractor's low-pressure tyres to function. The strip served a double purpose. Kitty was growing Kentucky bluegrass of the quick-spreading *Poa Poaceae* family. With strips remaining in the field, it would re-seed itself. If the first cutting were made early, a field might well be cut twice in one year.

Kitty checked her position carefully, on both sides and behind, then set her spotlights to work in front of her and dropped the blade. The weighted sheet of chrome steel slammed down into the earth to a depth of about four inches. Then, as the tractor moved the whole sled forward, the blade swivelled and began slicing at the bottom side of the grass roots. As the sod was cut it was forced up the curved section of the blade and picked up by the endless chain of the rotating carrier belt and dumped flat on the sled's polished top, where a second belt shook it loose from some of the precious topsoil, sliced it at the ten-foot mark, and forced it forward into the storage bin, where it coiled itself and was stored. A complete operation could be handled by one woman— if carefully done—on a perfectly graded field.

Every ounce of her concentration was needed to keep the machinery moving. There must be no slip, no variation from the plumb-line, no excess shaking or rolling or storing. Loading a bin of sod required as much effort and skill as juggling a dozen eggs while standing on one foot.

So it was no wonder when, squinting her eyes against the glare of the spotlights somewhat later, she saw a man standing directly in her path. With a groan of disgust she unshipped the clutch and brought the rig to a stop.

'You again?' She sighed as she stepped down from the cabin to stretch her legs. Her head was muzzy, her stomach unsettled.

'Hey, it's past midnight,' he replied, walking around to her side of the sled. 'Even the idle rich get concerned after a time. You've been running that machine——'

'Tractor,' she interrupted, making a wry face at him.

'You've been running that tractor for four hours, girl!'

'And if you'll kindly get out of my way I'll be running it for six hours more.' Her usually knife-like sarcasm failed her. She was too tired, and having trouble breathing.

'Surely it can wait until morning?'

'What are you, a member of the Subdivision Committee?' Kitty used one arm of her blouse as a towel, and wiped her forehead. 'For your information, Mr Harris has already been over here twice, telling me to stop the noise. It seems that Mrs Harris's bridge club is having trouble exchanging gossip!'

Joel grinned down at her and handed her a sealed container of some cool liquid. She could see the frost forming on the rim. 'I'm glad you said that, Kitty. I thought you just didn't like me, but now I see you don't like *anybody*. It makes things easier. Try some of this.' He stripped the cover from the container and handed it to her. She took a sip.

'Lemonade? My favourite.' She emptied the glass and handed it back to him. 'If it makes you feel better to think I'm the neighbourhood grouch, you go right ahead. Now, if you wouldn't mind getting out of my way?'

'How far could you have gotten with this if I hadn't dropped Mary off on you, Kitty?'

'I'd be finished about now,' she murmured.

'I have to admit it was a dirty trick,' he said. If she listened closely she could even hear a bit of remorse behind the words. 'But Mary can't stand anyone else in the house, and I just couldn't take her with me up to Taunton. How was I to know I lived next door to the only child-hater in the world?'

'I don't hate children.' Kitty sighed and flexed her stiffening shoulders. Somehow, perhaps because she was already dead tired, he no longer seemed the armoured knight, but rather a plain down-to-earth and caring neighbour. 'I just don't—have a great deal of interest in them. Now if you'll kindly get out of my way, I have to empty the bin before I cut another row.'

He walked past her to the sled itself. 'All this stuff that's rolled up in here? You're going to unload it?'

'If I could train the sod to jump on to the truck at a whistle-call, I'd have done it,' she muttered. 'Unfortunately I ran out of ideas when I completed the sled, so now I have to unload the stuff on to the pallets in the barn.'

'Now don't tell me that a little girl like you built this contraption?'

'Feel safe,' she assured him. 'I'm not about to undermine the entire male population's ego. I only designed the sled. Sampson & Ferry, the iron-works in Providence, built the machinery to my specifications.'

'You have a sharp tongue, Kitty.' He came back to her side and rested a hand on her sweat-soaked shoulder. 'But you might as well concede that you can't do away with the male entirely. He comes equipped with brute muscles. Watch me flex!'

'Oh, lord,' she muttered.

'And now I'm going to help you unload the bin. Did I get all the words right?'

He did. And considerably more than the words. The job that ordinarily took Kitty an exhausting hour was done in fifteen minutes. When the bin was unloaded Joel rode out to the field beside her, watching every move she made, questioning as she backed the sled back into the unfinished row, dropped the blade-edge, and began the cutting again.

'I wouldn't want to get caught under the edge of that thing,' he commented as they turned around at the end of the field.

Kitty was tired, and feeling a little dizzy, but it was pleasant to have someone with her, an interesting someone who could both talk and listen sensibly. 'It's the heart of the system. I got the idea from an old Hollywood movie,' she replied. 'They had a guillotine slicing off heads. That blade's my biggest trouble these days. I can't leave the sled outside for a minute —kids from the settlement come swarming over to play on it. Some day one of them is going to injure himself, and I can't afford the insurance.'

Four rows later, and another trip to unload the bins, and he was beginning to look as *she* felt. Contrary to all expectations, the temperature had dropped but a point or two from the daytime reading, and the dew point held steadily at seventy-nine point nine per cent.

'You don't have to stay,' she suggested as she gulped at the water-cooler in the barn. 'It's almost two o'clock in the morning. One more hour and I'll be finished, and then to bed.'

'A lonely bed?' he asked mournfully.

'Dear lord, don't you men ever think of anything else?' Kitty squared around to face him. 'Look at me. I'm soaked in sweat——'

'Perspiration,' he interrupted. 'Ladies don't sweat, they perspire.'

'Yeah,' she snarled. 'I'm up to my neck in—perspiration. I'm tired as a dog, my back hurts, my head hurts——'

'Not an opportune time to bring up sex, I suppose?'

'Quit while you're ahead, Mr Carmody,' she snapped as she climbed back on to the tractor and headed out to the field. 'I'd almost begun to like you!'

'Now that's a fine bit of progress,' he said. There was a silky soft tone in his voice that caressed her gently. She stole a quick look at him out of the corner of her eyes. He was sitting up straight, his arms folded in front of him, and had a very contented look on his face.

At four o'clock in the morning she turned the ignition key off for the last time, and looked around her. Each of the separate truck loads had been stacked, tagged, and dampened. The blade of the cutter had been washed and polished, and the sled itself had been sprayed clean by the hose. Her day was complete.

Joel was standing by the door, coiling the water-hose, when she came out of the barn, rubbing her nose.

'Itch?' he asked.

'Allergy,' she returned. 'I'm really not cut out to be a farmer.'

'So why keep at it, then?'

'First of all, because I had to clear the loan on the rest of the farm. The place really belongs to my brother Robert. Secondly, I need the money to carry on a search. I believe the old adage, "Don't get mad, get even." And when I find out who did all this to my brother, I intend to do just that—get even!'

She stopped to take a tortured breath. Anger was overwhelming her, as it did whenever she thought of her brother's departure. He had gone even before Kitty had arrived back in town to take over the work! 'And when I get even with those—with those people——'

'What people are those, Kit?' It all had such a friendly sound to it, and she was so tired, that she leaned back against him when he gave the slightest tug.

'Well, I don't know, do I?' she murmured. 'Somebody fouled up my brother's land deed, and weaselled out of the restrictive covenant. Somebody else either lied or did a poor job on the percolation tests over there. Someone did a fast cover-up of the entire affair. And when I find out who that someone is I'm going to singe his beard! After which——'

'Boy, a vengeance campaign,' Joel interrupted. 'But I'm interested in the other part too. Go ahead, you were saying, "after which"?'

'After which I'm going to write to my brother, and——'

'Write to him? Where is he now?'

'He's in the Sudan, with the Peace Corps. He'd contracted to go even before that darn bank foreclosed on his house. So he decided to go immediately, and come back afterwards to fight for the land! But I thought— well, I thought I might be able to work the land myself, and do some of the fighting for him.'

'All right, you've hung on to the land, and your brother comes home, and then what?'

'I'm going out and get myself a job as a computer-programmer. That's what I'm trained for. I'm going to live in air-conditioned rooms, eat steaks every day, and turn up my nose at Hopkins Neck. How's that for a daydream?'

'Not bad,' said Joel, chuckling. 'But it's almost four-thirty now——'

'And I have to be up by eight,' she murmured. 'Darn! You know, I have to lease these trucks by the hour and the mile. I—— Mr Carmody?'

'Joel. What?' His strong hands turned her gently around so that she was facing him. He was a tall dark shadow in a darker night, and she thanked the Lord for that. He couldn't possibly see the smile on her trembling cheeks, or the last little tear that ran down next to her aristocratic little nose.

'I—haven't been thinking nice thoughts about you— Joel. And I'm really sorry. Thank you for your effort tonight, and I've got to——'

'You've got to kiss me goodnight,' he murmured. 'That's standard pay for working after midnight, you know.' She didn't know, having never employed a male of the species in an after-hours job, so she tilted her head upward, pursed her lips, and felt the ghostly touch as he barely grazed her. But he was only firing to get the range, she thought hysterically a moment later. Those soft warm lips came back, made contact, pursued her deep inside herself, back to the little corner of her brain devoted to such things as thrills. And because the thrill was much bigger than the container to which she had assigned it, everything blew up, smashing flashes of light and noise all over her logical brain.

Some hours later, or so it seemed, she managed to grope her way back to sanity. Joel was holding her arms at the shoulder, and looking down at her quizzically. 'Thank you,' she whispered.

'Hey, that's my line,' he replied. 'I'm the one who got all the pleasure from it.'

'Did you?' Kitty was still too dazed to make sense out of anything. 'It seems that——' She swallowed and took a deep breath. 'It seems to me that I'd better lock the barn and get to bed. Goodnight, Mr—Joel.'

'Goodnight, Katherine Anderson.' The words seemed to float on the still air, hang there and multiply the pleasure. She walked the few steps to the back door of the house, happy. Joel stood by the open barn door and watched that strong little back, that lovely wobbling bottom, as they disappeared. Then he closed the barn door and flipped the padlock closed before walking slowly back up the hill.

Kitty made it to the house, and into the kitchen, where a single lamp gleamed over the kitchen table. I need a shower, she told herself. He's a nice man, even if his name *is* Carmody. Her head began to ache. She pushed the chair back and tried to walk to the bathroom. Somehow or another the floor shook beneath her feet. The walls seemed to vibrate as she held out her hands for support. Worried now, she reversed her direction and wobbled back towards her own bedroom.

Her head seemed to pound as if there were a rock band performing inside her ear. The floor made one or two more violent swaying movements, and Kitty collapsed and fell forward on to her bed. A wind began to rise outside, rattling at the loose front screen door. An owl hooted in the dimness of the trees around the brook. For the rest, there was silence.

Dawn came, brightly coloured, impatient. The sparrows that haunted the farm made a mockery of song. One car at a time, the inhabitants of the housing project began to filter out to their city jobs. All three of the leased trucks, small specialised vehicles prepared for the long haul, pulled off the road and parked in the empty space in front of the house.

Eight o'clock came and went. The drivers clustered. They had all brought coffee from the fast-food place in town, the black liquid still steaming in styrofoam cups. Joel Carmody came strolling down the hill, baby Mary strapped in a little canvas harness on his back.

'I thought you'd be all loaded and gone,' he said to the drivers.

'There don't seem to be nobody to home,' one of the men declared. 'Been running this Anderson trip for a year now. This is the first time there's nobody waiting for us.'

'Maybe she overslept,' Joel replied. 'Tell you what— there's no need to wake her up after such a short night. Everything's in the barn, waiting. You-all know what goes where?'

'Sure do,' they assured him. He walked as quietly as he could back around the house, then grinned at his own stupidity as the three trucks' engines roared and they began to follow him. 'Which ought to wake up the dead,' he assured the baby.

Mary thought it was a fine joke. She giggled and patted her uncle on top of his head. But then Mary was an unsophisticated audience. There was hardly anything Joel could do that didn't seem wonderful to his niece.

The trucks were already at the barn door when he arrived.

'Locked,' one of the men commented.

'Do you say so?' chuckled Joel as he reached into his pocket for his wallet, and produced the shining set of picks.

'Burglar tools,' one of the laconic drivers said. 'Get yourself arrested in Massachusetts just for carrying 'em.'

'Don't have any idea what you mean,' Joel returned. With an economy of motion he had the cheap padlock open before another comment could be made. The door swung back.

Within minutes each driver had identified his own load, and for the following twenty minutes there was a great deal of bustle in the back yard as the trucks were loaded. In another ten minutes the paperwork was complete, and, one at a time, the vehicles hit the road. Joel watched them go. Mary, bouncing on his back, was

waving a farewell and spouting a thousand indis-
tinguishable words.

'Yes, I think so too,' he assured the child as he tried
the front screen door. It was hooked on the inside by a
simple catch. He stopped for a moment to listen carefully. Nothing stirred, except for a late Cadillac climbing
up from the subdivision.

'Shall we?' he asked.

'Nuncle Joe,' the child responded, which he took to
be a total agreement. He used his petrol credit card. It
was stiffer than his other cards, and he needed it the
least. The screen door rattled as he pulled it open to the
limit of its hook. The card fitted into the empty space
between door and jamb, a slight pressure on the card
sent the hook flying, and the pair of them stepped inside.

'Kitty?' No response. The living-room looked as it had
on his first visit—neat, but not overly so. Everything in
order, as it should be. A little rim of dust could be seen
on the tops of things somewhat above the five feet high.
Especially on the upright piano. 'She said she wasn't the
most domestic woman in the world,' he assured Mary,
who hadn't been too concerned anyway. 'Kitty?' A little
louder. 'Kitty!'

The kitchen was a horse of a different colour. One
chair was overturned. The blouse she had been wearing
the previous night was on the floor. Shoes, separately
discarded, laid a trail to the back of the house, and by
that time Joel was standing at her bedroom door.

'Mama,' the child said. And there she was, sprawled
out on her bed, face down, dressed in not much more
than her dusty jeans. 'Oh, my God,' muttered Joel as
he unbuckled the canvas pack on his back and set Mary
down on the floor.

Kitty was breathing shallowly, making little bubbling
noises in her throat, but breathing. He squared her
around on the bed and turned her over. Her forehead

glowed. His questing hand felt more temperature than he liked. She was naked to the waist. He cautiously ran his hands down her sides, checking her ribs. Nothing seemed to be broken. When he moved his hands back up to her shoulders they trailed across her proud breasts without his approval. She stirred, moaned a protest, and then was stilled.

'Oh, my,' muttered Joel. The baby was standing quietly by the bed.

'Oh, my,' she imitated. 'Mama sick?'

'Mama's sick,' he murmured. He shifted Kitty's body far enough so that he could pull a sheet down, then cover her. 'Come on, love, we have to get a doctor.'

The pair of them wandered out into the kitchen. The telephone was hiding in the corner next to the stove. Attached to it was a small notebook of 'most often called' numbers. Joel's mind was running at full speed. There was a hospital in New Bedford, and one in Fall River. He could get her into an emergency room in perhaps an hour—or slightly more. Strangely enough, her family physician was listed as living in Taunton, the third city in the triangle that made up Bristol County. 'Rebecca Meadows, MD,' the book said. It was worth a try.

The dial rattled as Joel nervously stabbed a big finger into the little holes. The ring sounded several times, indicative that it was not in an office. After the fourth sounding the telephone on the other end was picked up, and a very young voice gave a hesitant, 'Hello.'

Puzzled, Joel asked, 'Is Dr Meadows available?'

'Mama? Sure. Just a minute.'

There was a pause, a sound of background movement, and a soft contralto voice answered. 'Dr Meadows?' he asked.

'Yes, but—who is this? I don't transact business from my home phone.'

'You wouldn't know me, Doctor. I'm Joel Carmody. I'm calling from the home of Kitty Anderson, down on Hopkins——'

'I know all about Kitty,' the doctor interrupted urgently. 'What's the trouble?'

He told her as best he could, but about halfway through his description the doctor stopped him again, with the most astonishing statement he had heard in years. 'I'll come to the house,' she said. 'I'll be leaving right away.'

Joel put the telephone down and went back to the bedroom. Kitty had hardly stirred. Her breath was still shallow. And he had no idea what to do about it. It hit him hard. As chairman of all the hundred or more Carmody retail food outlets he knew a great deal about market merchandising, food processing, shipping and administration. But with all his training, there was nothing he could do for this tiny little creature. Lacking any other thought, he pulled up a chair near the bed and held her hand. It was a comfort he had not expected. Little Mary ran around the house, searching, chattering, bubbling, until suddenly she fell over on to the thick rug in the bedroom and was instantly asleep.

Time seemed to have passed into slow motion. Occasionally Joel would lean over and wipe Kitty's dry forehead. His mind squirrelled. She was a lovely little woman. Unconscious, her face relaxed, showing a sort of beauty that was young and fresh and free. Her straw-blonde hair drooped over her cheeks, and he brushed it away. What sort of woman was she? Determined, rambunctious, angry—and she knew a doctor so well that there was to be a house call! It was something almost unheard of in the United States for a doctor to make a house call. He was checking his watch for the fourth time when the big Lincoln rolled up the entrance road and screeched to a stop. Two people got out—a tall, thin, black-haired woman, and a towering squarely built man who looked as if he might eat nails for breakfast.

The woman brushed him by with a brief 'Dr Meadows,' and went through to the bedroom.

The man stopped and offered a hand. 'Jake Meadows,' he said.

'Carmody,' Joel returned. 'And don't step on my niece, please,' he called after the woman, who acknowledged with a wave of her hand.

'I haven't seen you before,' remarked Jake as the two men walked slowly towards the bedroom. 'How are you related to Kitty?'

'No relative at all,' Joe said ruefully. 'But I suspect I'd like to be.'

'Boy, am I glad to meet up with you!' Jake said. 'We've been worried about Kitty for a year or more. She's a friend of the family, if you follow. Went to school with my wife's sister Faith.'

'High fever,' Dr Meadows reported. 'Vital signs aren't *too* bad. What happened, Mr—er——'

'Carmody,' her husband provided. 'The man we've been looking for, Becky. He *wants* to become a relative of Kitty's!'

'Stop it, Jake! Mr Carmody, tell me what happened.'

'Dr Meadows, yesterday was a bad day,' Joe reported slowly. 'She fell in the brook and got soaking wet. I gave her a hard time about my niece, and she became——'

'Angry will do—I know Kit very well. Call me Becky, by the way. So she was really teed off? And then what?'

'Then, about five o'clock or so, she came back down here alone, and started to cut sod in that upper field. When it got to midnight she was still at it, so I came down the hill and helped her finish. That would be about—oh, four o'clock. And then she went to bed. That's all I can tell you about last night. I watched the house for a minute, went back up the hill, and slept like a log.'

'And then this morning?'

'She told me the trucks would be here to load at about eight o'clock, so I came down at that time to see if I could help. The trucks were here, but there wasn't a sign of Katherine.'

'Katherine, is it?' The pair of them looked at each other and grinned. 'Did you know, Mr Carmody,' the doctor noted, 'that your niece sounds as if she might have a small problem with her adenoids? OK, what happened this morning?'

'Well, since I knew what was needed, I helped the truckers to load and saw them on their way, and there was still nothing stirring in the house. So I—er—managed to open the front screen door, and there she was, lying on her face on top of the bed.'

'What do you think, Becky?' asked Jake.

'Oh, it's just about what we should expect. She hasn't paid any attention to the pills I ordered for her the last time. It's been over a month, and there are only—one, two—two pills missing from the bottle. She hasn't even opened the second inhalator I sent her. I doubt if she's had a decent meal in all that time, either. Dear lord, she can't live on TV dinners all her life! I would say sheer exhaustion, coupled with an allergy reaction. Bronchial asthma. Maybe even a touch of pneumonia.'

'She *did* say something about allergies,' said Joel. 'When she came out of the barn last night. She was sneezing, and her eyes were watering.'

Becky shook her head in disgust. 'A woman with grass allergies runs a sod-farm! Dear lord, I could hit her with a telephone pole!' She was moving her stethoscope around on Kitty's chest. 'Yes, definitely some lung congestion. Just about what I suspected.'

'An allergy shot?' asked Jake. 'What she needs is two weeks in bed flat on her back, air-conditioning, decent meals—who in the world could handle her under *those* conditions?'

'Me,' Joel said quietly. Neither of them were listening.

'Hell, she doesn't even have electricity in the house,' Jake snorted. 'Hospital, for sure.'

'She won't like that,' Becky retorted. 'And she wouldn't stay very long. You know how she hates hospitals. I think she has a hospital allergy worse than her grass allergy!'

'I'll take care of it all,' Joel murmured.

'I'd love to leave her here, but that's impossible. She'll need to go in for a few days, at least. And then somehow if we could get her to relax, keep away from the grass. Damn, if there were just someone——'

'*Me!*' Joel shouted at them. 'Me!' This time both stopped and looked. 'I live up the hill. So when she comes back from the hospital we'll move her in with us—me and my niece. They're great friends, Mary and Kit. And I'll get the air-conditioners. And I've got the electricity. And I'll sit on her if she doesn't follow orders, and—what are the orders?'

'Good lord,' said Becky, examining him more closely, 'I thought the Sir Galahads were an extinct species.'

'Don't knock it,' her husband told her. 'When have you ever heard a better offer? If we follow the usual routine and send her to a hospital, we'll get her back on her feet, and as soon as she's out she'll be right back in the same old groove, and nothing will have been cured! A girl can't live on vengeance. I could kill that damn brother of hers, running away——'

'He had his problems too,' Becky interrupted. 'Not all of us have strong characters and firm determinations. Yes, I suspect you're right.' She turned to Joel. 'Now, Mr Carmody. She's sleeping, which isn't a bad thing. I'm going to give her a couple of shots. Then we'll call the ambulance and take her into—oh, I guess New Bedford will be better. Give her a few days in hospital, and then, if she doesn't make too much of a fuss, you can take her home with you. Are you sure you can——?'

'I'm sure,' Joel responded. 'I can get plenty of help.'

'You realise that I just gave you some contrary orders? Keep her in bed and don't let her get excited? It won't be easy. She hates a great many things.'

'I know,' Joel told her. 'Among her thousand and one hates is me. And she hates my family, for some reason that I'm still exploring. But I'll keep a heavy hand on her, believe me.'

'That's the way,' said Jake. 'Firm hand. Take no nonsense. Women need to be kept in their place!'

'Oh, shut up,' his wife told him with a smile. 'You talk more nonsense per square yard than any other doctor I've ever been married to!' They were still arguing amiably as they went out to the kitchen to call the ambulance.

Joel shook his head as he looked at the array of pills on Kitty's bedside table, and then back at the relaxed face of the little woman who had suddenly become a major interest in his life.

'Mary,' he asked, looking down at his niece on the floor, 'do you really have trouble with adenoids?' The little girl rolled over on her stomach and burped lightly, but didn't answer.

CHAPTER FOUR

'YOU again?' The grumpy voice from the bed belied the smile Kitty was trying to hide. The hospital gown did nothing for her, but her long blonde hair swirling in an awful mess over her face provided a place to hide.

'Me again,' he said as he pulled up a chair. 'Joel M Carmody, at your service.'

'I've been here seven days, and you've come in every day!' It came out like an accusation, but Kitty didn't really mean it that way. He was an important visitor. In fact, except for her lawyer and her doctor, he was her *only* visitor. Rogers Ward was not the newest part of St Luke's Hospital, but it stored its patients two to a room, and if the other bed were empty, as it was in Kitty's case, it could be a lonely sort of existence.

'That's because they won't let me come mornings, and I can't find a night-time baby-sitter for Mary,' Joel explained. 'I see you're your usually cheery self today.'

'I am not,' she snapped. 'I'm never cheerful.' And just for a moment a tear or two escaped. Because it was true, frankly, and because she could remember when it hadn't been so. Kitty Anderson had once been as light-hearted and laughter-filled as anyone could ask, until her brother ran out on her. And that, she reminded herself, was the first time she had used the phrase 'ran out on her'! She wasn't *admitting* it, but she had thought the phrase!

'I brought you some flowers this time,' he said, laying a bunch of violets down on the pristine white sheet.

She jerked away as if the little cluster of beauty concealed a rattlesnake. 'You know I can't have flowers,' she said hoarsely. 'I'm allergic to them!'

'Well, that's OK—they're artificial. Pretty little things, aren't they?'

'I—yes. I'm sorry.' He towered over her, an imposing broth of a man, Kitty thought. It wouldn't be smart to be caught lying down when this fellow's around. Or would it? The idea made a delicious puzzle and lightened her spirits.

'No need to be sorry. How do we feel today?'

'We?' she queried.

'Hey, I don't have a lot of hospital experience, but I've been listening at doors as I came by. People don't say to the patient "How are *you* feeling?" Never. It's always "How are *we* feeling?"'

It was almost impossible to hide the smile now. 'In that case, *we* are feeling a lot better. In fact, *we* feel well enough to go home and get back to work.'

Joel grinned down at her. 'It doesn't seem that *we* have been paying much attention to what the doctor said. She said *we* weren't going to go back to work for some time. In fact, tomorrow morning *we* are going to come home to *my* house and spend two weeks relaxing.'

'Over my dead body!' snapped Kitty.

'I guess that could be arranged, but Mary wouldn't like it. She's looking forward to renewing acquaintances. The house will be practically empty, you know. Just you and I and Mary and the cook. And—oh yeah, my brother John and his wife Jessica.'

'That snob?'

'I'm not sure which one of them you mean. But let's face it, girl, you're the worst snob in Northport. My brother might have been, but you take the prize right out of his hands!'

It didn't seem proper to stick her tongue out at him. She leaned back against the pillows. 'I can't take time off now,' she muttered. 'I must have four dozen orders waiting to be filled. I've got to get back to the cutting. This is the height of the season for sod-farming.'

'Mule-headed.' Joel held up both hands defensively in front of him when she started to protest. 'Mule-headed! That's what your doctor said. A very straight-forward lady, that one. You needn't worry—you had three dozen and six orders waiting, and I cut the whole thing this week. All the shipments have gone out, and we had only one complaint.'

'Oh, no! You didn't cut the south field? Don't tell me you did!'

'I'm sorry to tell you I did,' he reported. His face wore that hangdog look one found on a cheerful Great Dane. 'That was the most physical labour I've done in years.'

Which left Kitty with several things she wanted to know, and she was not quite certain how to go about asking them. 'The complaint?' she asked hesitantly.

'The builder up in Nashua,' he said. 'I—well, being a salesman myself, I told him that the lot we furnished did better in cool weather.'

'And now you're a sod expert? How in the world——?'

'You labelled it Canadian Bluegrass,' he explained. 'Obviously Canadian bluegrass is bound to grow better up north than Kentucky bluegrass. He agreed with me and asked for another five hundred linear feet.'

Kitty sighed. 'Oh boy! I hope it grows. That's *Poa Compressa*—a European import. But when you say—what you said there—real fast, it almost sounds logical, even to me.'

He gave her an injured look, but his muscles could not stand the strain. Injury broke down into a wide grin that stretched from ear to ear and displayed his splendid teeth. And he waited.

Darn the man, she thought, biting her lip. He knows I want to ask something else, and he's daring me! Talk about gall!

'It must have been hard work,' she said primly. 'And I'm surprised that you could do it. What *do* you do for a living? Some corporate job in the family, you said?'

'Why, I thought everybody knew,' he replied. 'I used to be in the detection business, but now I run a grocery store.'

'A detective? In Kentucky?'

'Private eye!' His laugh filled the room. 'Around Paducah, Louisville. In those parts. Like that.'

'A grocery store?'

'Why do I get the opinion that every time I tell you something you don't believe it?'

'Because it sounds so preposterous. Look at you, a giant of a man. You've more muscles than you know what to do with! I just can't see you standing behind a counter!'

'Thank you, ma'am.' And now he's laughing again, Kitty raged to herself. Look at the man! Doing his best not to show it! I ought to lean over and give him a good whack!

What really disturbed her, though, was that she leaned in his direction, raised her right hand to his cheek, and found herself *stroking* it! Stroking his cheek! She covered the blush and the withdrawal with a coughing spell, and, when the subterfuge was over, there he was sitting tall, with that phoncy 'sincere' look on his face.

'Groceries can get mighty heavy when you deal with family-sized orders,' he pontificated.

'You need a shave,' she muttered, trying another defensive ploy. Joel scratched at his own chin.

'Right you are. I usually shave before I visit the ladies—but I had no idea we were going to get this close! Now what else do you want to know? Where I come from, we tend to come right out in the open with our questions.' All followed by that meek little 'church-mouse' smile of his, that aggravated her more than words!

'All right!' She pushed the button on the side of her bed to raise herself into a sitting position. Being flat on your back was too much of a disadvantage with this man around. 'Your brother——'

'John. His name is John. My brother John.'

'Yes, John. What does *he* do for a living?'

'Ah, John. You haven't met him before?'

'No, but then I haven't gone looking for any Carmodys. Not yet, that is.'

'My, that sounds ominous! Let's see—my little brother John. Well, we have more than one store, you see. John lives out there on the Neck, and runs the New England end of the business.'

'And that's all he does? He isn't a detective, too?'

'Good lord, no! John couldn't find his mouth on a sunny day!'

Kitty looked up at him speculatively, then hid under her long eyelashes. 'You don't suppose he's in real estate?'

'I guess I can't answer that question, Kitty.' He had become serious again; the teasing repartee was gone. 'I haven't kept as close an eye on the operations up here as I should have. I came two weeks ago for a family pow-wow about Mary, and now there seem to be all sorts of other problems.' He got up from his chair and strolled over to the window, keeping his back to her, hands in his pockets.

Kitty took a deep breath. All her suspicions were back—all of them. And they hurt. They clashed against all the little tender memories of Joel which she had absorbed in the past few days. Little pictures, teasing her with affection, jumbled now with all the bad things she suspected. But she *had* to know!

'So I don't suppose you know who's responsible for building the subdivision across from my house!'

He turned around, and she could see the bleak expression on his face. 'I never knew it existed until the day I met you. I'm having some enquiries made. It's an interesting little problem. You said they were polluting your well. How about their own water supply?'

'Town water.' She almost exploded with the violence of her anger. 'Tax-payers' money ran a water pipe down that road, and I can't afford to tap in on it!'

'Hey, no excitement! Doctor's orders.' One of his hands was holding hers gently, while the other brushed through her mop of hair. Kitty caught her breath and regained control.

'I'm doing some investigating too,' she said in a flat, lustreless tone. 'And when I find out who's responsible, Mr Carmody, I'm going to cloud up and rain all over him! I think you'd better go.'

'I think I'd better,' he agreed. 'One of the doctor's instructions was not to get you excited.'

'I'm *not* excited!' He saw her eyes gleam, heard her teeth grate, sensed the tense muscles beneath the white cotton sheet. 'I *never* get excited!'

But by that time he was up and at the door, throwing a cheery 'g'day' in her direction. His hands were still in his pockets, and she heard him whistling gently as he walked down the corridor. Considering her lack of experience with men, it was not surprising that she didn't recognise the noise as 'whistling past the graveyard'.

Kitty lay back on her pillows for a moment, trying to calm down. The girl who 'never got excited' had been within a ace of braining him with her water-jug. And at the same time another part of her mind was saying something of the order of 'How nice it is for him to come, and to make all that effort to cut sod for me! He could easily have broken his back!' And the big question followed: 'Is that love?' But for that she had no answer.

Puzzled at her own confusion, she struggled up out of bed and wobbled over to the bathroom. When she came out, she had another visitor.

'Faith! Good of you to come see me.'

'Business,' her lawyer said. 'How come you're out of bed?'

'I'm going home tomorrow,' Kitty boasted.

'And did you pay attention to the rest of the restrictions?'

'Faith, your sister is an old stick-in-the-mud!' Kitty complained.

'Becky is the best doctor in the county. Well, maybe second-best. Jake's one fine doctor too.'

'OK, OK,' sighed Kitty. 'I don't want to get the whole Latimore family down on my head. What's the business?'

'I'm glad you said that about the family,' Faith said, laughing. 'Ma was talking about coming down here and taking you in hand! Oh, the business—yes. We won our plea in Superior Court this morning. The town *has* to show us all pertinent percolation tests, and all deeds and covenants relating to the subdivision. That's step number one.'

'Step number one? That's all the steps there are!' Kitty exclaimed in high glee.

'Whoa! It's not that easy. I have the suspicion that the town is going to stall and whimper and plead for as long as they can get away with it. But we'll keep after them. I've found an investigator and an accountant to work on the case——'

'Oh, lord, I can't afford that. The only reason I can afford *you* is because you come for free!'

'Not to worry,' the pert, willowy blonde said. 'We've received a donation from a private citizen to help support the cause.'

'Oh, no, not your father!' groaned Kitty.

'Pop swears he has nothing to do with it. The donation was anonymous and in cash. I'd even forgotten whose face was on the one-hundred-dollar bill!'

'Don't tell me,' Kitty said, her spirits somewhat restored. 'I don't want to become accustomed to that rich kind of conversation.'

'Now,' said Faith, ignoring her comment completely, 'what we really need is a good undercover investigator to sneak into a few places and——'

Kitty was too excited to keep a secret. 'Like the Carmody house?'

'Like the Carmody house? Better still the Randolph house. Do you know something about the Carmodys that I don't know?'

'Randolph? I don't understand,' Kitty replied, puzzled. 'He's just the banker.'

'He's also the first selectman,' Faith reminded her, 'And chairman of the Department of Public Works. There's a political mouse in our woodpile. So tell me, what else is on your mind?'

'I'm going home tomorrow. Becky arranged it. Or maybe it was Jake. I'm going to spend two or three weeks convalescing.'

'So drop the other shoe,' prompted Faith.

'I'm going to do my convalescing in the Carmody house. How about that?'

'Becky arranged that? That's where you're going to have all this peace and quiet? That's where you're not going to get excited? My sister must have rocks in her head! And you agreed?'

'After a while I did. Think about it, Faith. There I'll be, little old inoffensive me, invalided out, weak, trembling, trusting to the broad shoulders of Joel Carmody to protect me from the world!'

'I'm thinking,' her lawyer drawled, 'and it makes me feel like upchucking. I have the suspicion that there's more to this than what you say. You wouldn't be planning an all-out affair with this Joel Carmody?'

'Faith!' Kitty looked up anxiously. 'We went all through school together, and that's what you think of me?'

'I saw him down in the lobby,' said Faith. 'He's some dish. But look, Kit, do you think he's going to have some incriminating papers hidden away behind his socks in the bureau? Dear lord, Kitty, you don't have the brains to come in out of the rain!'

'I've read a lot of spy stories,' Kitty maintained grimly. 'I can do it, and I'm going to!'

Her lawyer shook her head in disgust as she pulled out her pen. 'Stubborn as a mule,' she replied. 'Sign here.'

Joel was as true as his word. He appeared at eight o'clock, right in the middle of start-up procedures on the hospital day-shift. 'She can't leave until the doctor signs her out,' the nurse insisted. 'You have to wait in the lobby until then. She has to dress, and get packed, and——'

'You don't know with whom you're dealing,' said Joel. They were standing in the doorway of Kitty's room. She could hear it all, but could not see. She hitched herself up in her bed and eavesdropped unabashedly. 'Look, this woman is a suspect in a series of crimes all over South-eastern Massachusetts. You leave her one little mouse-hole and she'll escape before you can blink an eye. That's what I'm here for, see?'

He must have shown the nurse something conclusive, because she admitted him immediately, then watched the pair of them out of the corner of her eyes as she went about the business of posting charts.

'Good morning, Katherine,' said Joel pleasantly.

'What did you show her?' Kitty hissed.

'Show her? My patented smile? My "you can trust this man" stance. Whatever happened to the "good morning" routine?'

'You're up to something, Joel Carmody, and I intend to find out what. Besides giving me a bad reputation, what else?'

'I wouldn't do a thing like that, Kit, not unless it was absolutely necessary! So perhaps I embroidered the truth a little, but I did that for *her* sake. Nurses lead a depressing life. I was only trying to make her day for her. Oh, and I showed her my badge.' He reached into his shirt pocket and brought out a polished gold badge. 'Health Inspector,' it said. 'Paducah, Kentucky.'

Kitty fell back into her pillows and sighed. 'You've got more brass than my grandfather's spittoon. I don't want to go home with you. I don't trust you!'

'Good morning?'

'Good morning.' It came reluctantly, but it came.

'You're glad to see me—c'mon, say it.'

'My throat hurts.' She coughed to demonstrate.

'I've heard better coughs than that. C'mon, you're glad to see me.'

'I'm—er—glad,' she stopped for another cough, then raced through the last of the phrase, 'to see you.'

'See, that didn't hurt, did it?'

You've no idea how much, Kitty thought as she manufactured another little smile. 'I still don't trust you. And now I have to get dressed,' she maintained.

'I brought you something—went down to your house and made a selection for you. Sure you'll like it.'

'Put it on the bed.' She held her grimace back until he had gone. The man's taste was obviously all in his mouth, she assured herself as she looked at the collection. The orange blouse she had bought for a Hallowe'en party and hadn't the nerve to wear even then. A pair of red-white-and-blue striped trousers she had worn for the two-hundredth anniversary celebration of the United States' birthday. A pair of white court shoes old enough to recall the Battle of Bunker Hill. She shrugged her shoulders as she struggled into it all. Even the nurse laughed as she finally finished her charting, winked at Kitty, and went out into the corridor. Joel came back in.

'Lovely,' he gloated. 'I've always had an eye for what clothes a woman looks good in.'

'Or out of,' Kitty said coolly.

'My goodness, we *are* sharp this morning!' He loaned her an arm. She needed it; the brief excursion out of bed had left her a little dizzy. 'I met your doctor in the hall. Let's go. I've posted your bail bond.'

'That's not what they call it in a hospital,' she snapped. 'It's called a bill, and I don't know how I am going to pay for it. Farmers don't get health insurance for their labours.'

'I persuaded them to let you pay it off on the instalment plan,' he told her. 'A dollar a week for two centuries—something like that.' There was something more that Kitty could have added, but the nurse came back in at that moment with the wheelchair, and she was beginning to feel just the slightest bit embarrassed about her own bad temper. Having shut her mouth, she kept it shut through the whole trip until Joel's car, an air-conditioned Mercury, pulled up in front of his house.

Carswell answered the first ring of the bell, as if he had been standing there, peering out of the little chapel window set in the wall beside the door. 'Madam.' He managed a quarter bow. Which is certainly better than my last reception, Kitty thought. I'm going up the ladder!

'Any problems, Carswell?' asked Joel.

'The—er—child, Mr Carmody.'

'Yes? Her aunt Jessica agreed to watch her.'

'Unfortunately, sir, the child cannot abide Mrs Carmody. She screamed and kicked for an hour, until the lady rushed out of the door and drove off in a fury.'

'Dear lord, can't *anybody* in this family handle a baby?' demanded Joel.

'Apparently not,' the butler condescended. 'I took the liberty of putting the child in the nursery and closing the door—sir.'

'Damn! With as many traumas as that child has, you shut her up in the nursery? It seems that none of you people know who you're working for,' Joel snapped as he headed for the stairs. 'It's *my* house; *I* pay all the salaries!' He bounded up the stairs two at a time. Kitty, exhausted by her little trip, walked over to the stairs and sat down on the second tread. Joel's remarks had evidently startled the butler. He stood there at the bottom of the stairs, one foot still up in the air, then turned and dashed for the living-room. In her tired and confused state Kitty heard the clink of a glass and the gurgle of liquid. Carswell needs liquid courage, she thought as she leaned back against the newel post. What a house!

She was still in this slightly dizzy state, staring at the hall carpet, when another pair of shoes came into her line of sight. 'And who might *you* be?' a voice said.

Kitty's head was not quite secure on her shoulders. She tilted it up carefully until her eyes focused on a face. There was some familiarity to it. He looked to be the completely new model, perfectly manufactured, of the Joel figure. A broad face, unruffled. No scars, no bumps, of which Joel had a few. An aristocratic nose, but of proper proportion. And he stood, at a guess, some three or four inches taller than Joel. And so he must be——

'I'm John Carmody,' he said. 'This is my house.' And then he repeated, 'And who might you be?'

'I might be most anybody.' Kitty sighed. It was hard to keep her mind on her business. Being the meanest woman in town was not something you did in your off-hours. It took considerable amounts of concentration. But the best she could offer at the moment was a very weak, 'Your brother brought me here.'

'My brother brought you here?'

'There's a terrible echo in this hall, did you know? You need more carpets, or wall-hangings—something like that.' Her neck was too tired to hold her head up. Kitty went back to her floor-watching.

'I might have known!' the man said, disgusted. 'Joel drags all kinds of waifs into the house, and doesn't pay any attention to what the neighbours might say. I have a reputation to maintain!'

'I'm sure you do,' Kitty murmured. 'But you needn't worry on my account. I *am* the neighbours, and I won't say a thing—honest.' She had worked out another witticism, but footsteps thundered on the stairs above her as Joel came running down and interrupted her train of thought.

'Just what the hell is going on here?' asked John. His brother shot him one steely look before he stooped down and swept Kitty up in his arms.

'Go soak your head,' Joel advised as he ran back up the stairs again, carrying Kitty in his arms. And that, Kitty thought drowsily, is what bothers me. He runs *up* the stairs carrying me? Even Errol Flynn couldn't do that on his best movie day! And he works in a grocery store? It was a tangle she could not work out.

Joel pushed at a half-open door and carried her across the threshold of a large bedroom. Kitty opened one eye, just to satisfy her curiosity. The ceiling was gold—or golden. Her other eye came open defensively. There were cherubs painted into the corners, and a huge Emperor bed standing with its head to the outer wall, between two enormous windows. But at least when he got to the bed, instead of lowering her gently, he dropped her on to the bouncy mattress and breathed a sigh of relief. It was good to know that he wasn't actually a superman!

'Out of condition?' she muttered.

'Probably,' he panted. 'Look, I'm sorry, but we have to do a little time-sharing. The nursery is under construction, so I had Mary's crib put in your sitting-room alcove. It won't be for long.' A little alarm bell began to ring in the back of her mind. His hand slipped under her back and lifted her. She heard the sheets being pulled back, and then moments later he was working at the buttons of her blouse. Share with the baby? She made a feeble effort to brush him off, with no success. Her head dropped back on the pillow and her fingers plucked at the casing.

For a grocery clerk Joel knew a great deal about packaging. She could feel the cool winds of an air-conditioner blow over her as he very efficiently stripped her and then gently pulled a nightgown over her head. 'What are you doing?' she managed to spit out.

'Just what the doctor ordered,' he reported as he pulled the sheet back up over her and tucked her in. 'Bed-rest, no excitement, and like that.'

'I don't trust you.'

'Hey!' Her eyes were closed, but she could imagine that big grin all the same. 'I never would have believed that. Go to sleep, Katherine.'

She struggled against the need. It wasn't true that she didn't trust him. She did. What bothered her was that she couldn't understand *why* she trusted him, and before she could find out she fell asleep.

*   *   *

The house faced west, looking out over the cliffs and the ocean. When the dancing sunbeams struck Kitty's eyes she jerked away and tried to sit up. It all came back to her in a flash. The Carmody house, being carried upstairs, being—undressed. Tough little Kitty Anderson could not control the blush that swept over her.

She rolled over slightly. There was a rattling noise from the alcove room behind the curtain, and a thump as something hit the floor heavily. The curtain wavered and parted as little Mary, dressed only in a nappy, came waddling out into the sunlight.

'Mama!' the child squealed. In her haste she stumbled, fell flat on her face, managed to elevate herself and came hurrying to the bed.

'It's impossible for her to climb up here,' Kitty told herself. But she had reckoned without the little stool at her bedside. The child swarmed up like an accomplished mountain-climber, stumbled across the uneven sheets, and dived head-first, ending up with her perspiring little head resting on Kitty's breast.

'Mama,' the child sighed as she wriggled for a moment and then relaxed. Kitty groaned and let herself slide back into the blankets. The child wiggled a little on to her stomach, secured a more comfortable place for her head, and dropped off to sleep again.

Oh, brother, Kitty thought. He's doing it to me again! I am *not* going to fall for that ploy about 'everybody loves my niece!' I am *not* going to do that! But despite her determination, she knew it wasn't true.

There was a certain comfort to having the little girl there. Her soft russet hair, fine as silk, was a comfort to brush against. She breathed partly through her mouth, with a little whistle that was not the least offensive. She was lying on her stomach, with her knees tucked underneath her. As a result, her cute little bottom made a sort of mountain that wiggled with every breath. And so when

Joel came in the door and started to say something Kitty said, 'Sh!'

He grinned at her as he walked across the room and knelt by the bedside. 'Time she woke up,' he murmured, 'or she won't sleep at all tonight.'

His soft voice was enough. The baby stirred, rolled over on her back, looked over at him, and jumped up. And I wish I had a self-starter like that, Kitty told herself. The little girl crawled across the bed, bumping a time or two on Kitty's stomach, and was swept up in his arms. 'Nuncle Joe,' the child burbled as she cuddled against his neck.

See that? Kitty chided herself. It's a universal feeling. Every female in the world wants to cuddle on his shoulder! And she blushed again, because there was no doubt in her mind that jealousy drove her to such thoughts.

'It's five o'clock,' said Joel. 'I'm accustomed to country suppers. Think you could come downstairs?'

'Of course I can. I'm no invalid. Just because I slept an hour——'

'More like five,' he interjected.

'So make a liar out of me over a few minutes,' she snapped. 'I have to get dressed.'

'Yes,' he commented. He was busy rubbing the little girl's back, and made not a motion towards the door.

'I *have* to get dressed,' Kitty repeated.

'Yes, you said that.'

'Then why the devil don't you have the courtesy to get out of my room?'

Joel shook his head slowly, and the baby giggled. 'It's not funny, Mary. Your uncle is a dummy. Of course. Get out of your room. My room, to be technical about it, but that doesn't matter. We'll wait in the hall. I had everything in your cupboards brought over while you were asleep.'

Kitty watched them go with hands folded over her breasts to keep from throwing something. How in the world can you maintain a good honest anger when the man won't fight back? she thought. Every time I insult him he smiles! I could learn to really *hate* a man like that! I really could. And then, hesitantly—it can't possibly be love!

She was still talking to herself as she went through her clothing, hung neatly on racks in the walk-in cupboard. Selecting something for supper wouldn't be too difficult; there just wasn't a great deal to choose from. With that depressing thought hanging over her head like a dark storm-cloud she opted for a simple white blouse buttoned up the front, and a wrap-around skirt of navy-blue.

As always her hair was the problem. It would curl no matter what she desired, refuse to be forced into anything more stylish than a braid. Because of her peaches and cream skin her straw-blonde tresses stood out like a flaming beacon. Discouraged, she brushed it until it sparkled, then fastened it at the nape of her neck with a spare shoestring.

'Now that, Mary, is prompt. Fully dressed in only fifteen minutes!' Joel was sitting on the top stair, watching as the baby ran back and forth in the upstairs corridor. When Kitty came over he rose and swept the child up.

'Pretty,' he said as he looked Kitty over from top to bottom.

'Priddy,' the little girl agreed. Kitty, who assumed that neither of them could see well, sniffed and went on down the stairs.

The family dining-room was located just beyond the drawing-room, on the first floor. John Carmody was standing at a built-in bar at the far end of the room. His flushed face indicated that he had been there for some time. His wife Jessica stood directly in front of him, a wine glass in her hand. She looked as if the lecture of the day had just concluded. When John cleared his throat and nodded towards the door the pair of them turned to look.

'Ah, Miss—er——'

'Anderson,' Kitty provided the missing piece, and offered him a sweet little smile, which seemed to set him off balance.

'Yes. Miss Anderson. I didn't realise just who you were. My wife tells me we're next-door neighbours. Care for a drink?'

'Whisky sour,' Kitty said out of habit.

'Orange juice,' countermanded Joel. 'You can't drink alcohol on top of those pills the doctor prescribed.'

'But I——' Kitty had whirled around to glare at him, but the look he gave her was enough to singe a buffalo hide. 'Yes—I've always wanted orange juice,' she concluded. A moment later, drink in hand, she managed to manoeuvre John into a corner.

'They tell me you deal with everyone in Bristol County,' she proposed as she raised her glass to toast him. 'Do you know anyone in real estate?'

'Real estate? Me?' He appeared dumbfounded, and might have added something worth hearing, except that his wife, finding her little lamb had been cut out of the flock, whisked over to his side and nudged him, not too gently.

'Real estate,' he pondered. 'Oh yes, real estate. I handle so many lines, you see, that it's sometimes hard for me to remember them all. And what do *you* do, Miss Anderson?'

'Oh, this and that. I'm an agriculturalist, mainly.'

'An——?'

'She's a farmer,' his wife cut in. 'She runs that farm down below us, John. You remember Mr Anderson, her father?'

'Oh yes, Mr Anderson. How is your father these days?'

And that does it! Kitty told herself angrily. A fine package, this man, but nothing inside. I've never talked into a complete vacuum before! 'My father is as well as can be expected,' she replied. 'He died almost three years ago.'

A look of pain shot across John's face. 'Died, huh? I'm sorry to hear that. Death diminishes us all, doesn't it?'

'You'll have to excuse my husband,' Mrs Carmody said. 'He's a very sensitive man.'

Yes, and you're not, Kitty thought. Jessica Carmody was the sort of cool executive woman who passed through life without any of it—especially the dirt—actually clinging to her. About five feet seven, thin to the point of starvation, she wore her silver lamé dress with a flair. Her brown hair glistened, as did the diamond clip she wore to keep it off her forehead. Kitty fought back the impulse to grab at the clip and run to scratch the window glass with it, to see if it were genuine.

'Dinner is served,' Carswell announced. They moved to the dining-room across the hall. There were only four chairs set. Joel and Jessica sat facing each other, like participants in a duel. John took a seat to his wife's left. Kitty took the remaining chair, sitting back and straight, to keep out of the line of fire. The baby bounced on Joel's knee.

If ever a patriarch looked like the prophet of doom, Joel Carmody did just at that moment. When he spoke it was with a soft, gentle voice, but anyone with sense could feel the steel that lay beneath. 'I thought,' he said, 'that we had agreed we would always set a place for Mary.'

'She's only a baby,' Jessica replied. Kitty winced at the sharpness in her voice. 'We can't be sharing a table with a baby! For heaven's sake, Joel, why don't you do the right thing? Hire a nanny for the kid, let her eat in the nursery or in the kitchen, and stop acting like a deprived father!'

For the moment Joel ignored her. He turned around to Carswell and made a commanding motion. The butler frowned, but quickly obeyed. A moment later a middle-aged woman enveloped in a large apron came in with a baby-chair, which she set at Joel's elbow, between himself and Kitty. 'There,' the woman said, 'I always said children should eat with their families.'

'That's strange, Mrs Wright,' Joel replied bleakly, 'that's what I've always said myself.' Then he turned on his sister-in-law. 'Now I don't intend to repeat myself, Jessica. This is *my* house, Mary is *my* niece. She's going to eat with the family. If you don't feel you can agree, why, perhaps you and John can go out and get your own house, have your own meals together—hell, maybe even raise your own children!'

Jessica Carmody turned red in the face and snatched up her napkin to dab at her eyes 'John,' she said bitterly, 'are you going to let him talk to me like that?'

John Carmody turned towards his wife for the first time, his mouth cut like a grim slash straight across his face. 'Maybe I should have talked to you like that myself,' he said. 'My big brother seems to know more about a lot more things than I do!'

'Oh, for heaven's sake!' his wife snapped. She pushed her chair back, watched it topple over on the floor, and stalked out of the room. 'I don't have to share meals with pigs,' she announced as she swept out of the door. A moment of silence followed.

'Eat your soup, Kitty,' murmured Joel. Another moment of silence, and then, 'You need to be more firm with her, John.'

'I know,' his brother replied. 'But it's not easy. Sometimes she's not well.'

'Neither is Katherine,' said Joel, 'and I don't intend for her to be the target in all these little domestic difficulties.' Kitty could feel his soft warm eyes on her, but didn't know what to say. She turned back to her soup.

CHAPTER FIVE

KITTY spent the next five days building up her strength. Joel stayed with her all day for the first three days, but then, noting her improvement, disappeared about his business—whatever that was. She improved her exercise schedule with short walks in the sunshine, the first for no more than ten minutes, the third for a full hour, until she managed to work her way along the ridge to the point where river and ocean clashed. She was sitting in the shade of a granite outcropping on that fifth afternoon when a four-wheel-drive vehicle pulled up behind her.

Her neck was too stiff to make the complete turn in their direction, so she waited patiently until the two men walked over to her. Joel, dressed casually in T-shirt and shorts, was with a man in a neat brown suit whom she had never met before.

'Katherine, this is Lieutenant Frankel, of the State police,' he said.

She nodded, regretting the fragile beauty of the world which the approach of the two men had destroyed. 'I thought State policemen all wore dark glasses and jack-boots?' Even to herself that sounded too crude. Strange, how much she was noticing about herself these days. 'I'm sorry, Lieutenant.'

He grinned at her. 'We do, but only at night when we're on television programmes.' He didn't look like a trooper—hardly five feet nine, with a receding hairline, wearing gold-rimmed glasses. He did look fit, but not exceptionally so.

'Straight ahead there,' Kitty pointed dreamily into the hazy distance. 'England, three thousand miles. I wish I were there. Or in Oz. Did you come to daydream too?'

'Not exactly, ma'am. I'm with the district attorney's investigations division.' He moved into the shade on her right, and settled himself back against the rock as he wiped his forehead. 'Phew, it's hot! I've never seen a hotter summer.'

'Or more humid,' she agreed. 'Having a crime wave, are we?'

Joel dropped down to the ground on her left and touched the top of her nose with his index finger. 'We're being serious, Kit.'

'I'm always serious, Joel. Hadn't you noticed?' She managed to turn her head far enough to stare at him. 'I strained my neck somehow or other—racing with your niece and those two darn dogs yesterday, I think. I was planning to go into Fall River to see a chiropractor.'

'You can think of more excuses to go than a dog has fleas.' He chuckled as his hand caressed the back of her neck, then dug into the overtight muscles at her nape in a gentle massage. 'But the doctor still says no. In fact, I think you've come too far today—all alone too.'

'I'm not all alone!' Kitty spluttered at him. 'Your damn—darn—mutt wouldn't let me go by myself.' She gestured down the steep incline that led to the sea. 'The one you call Honey. Hung to my footsteps like a prison warden, then ran off to catch seagulls as soon as I sat down. Now stop bugging me and get to business. I'm sure you didn't drive all the way down the Neck just to wish me good day!'

'Although it wouldn't be a bad idea,' the lieutenant mused as he plucked a grass stem and began chewing on it. 'No, Miss Anderson, I've come on another matter. Last night somebody came to your farm to make trouble. According to witnesses they hung a dummy on your apple tree and set fire to it, then they threw a brick through your window with a note attached.'

'They thought I was at home?'

'We don't know that, Miss Anderson. But the last time a crime was committed down here on the Neck was in 1938, when a couple of immigrants started a battle royal. So I thought I might come and have a talk with you. Do you know anyone who has a grudge against you?'

'I can't say that I know anyone by name,' Kitty replied cautiously. Her mind began to get up to speed. Somebody with a grudge? Outside of the whole population of Northport, that was to say?

'How about this?' Joel pulled a folded newspaper out of his back pocket. The weekly *Northport News*, with a banner headline: 'Local Woman Sues Selectman!' Kitty snatched it out of his hand and unfolded it. The story was brief, not exactly the entire truth, but it did mention the freedom of information suit, and the court order to the town. It also listed all the things that *might* happen, ranging from gaol if some official were caught with his hand in the till, to the possible requirement for the subdivision on the Neck to pay for sewer services and other penalties.

'I hadn't thought about *that* part,' Kitty said, pointing to the subdivision's connection. 'But then there aren't any hard-working middle-class people living there. They all can afford sewers. I don't see any reference to the idea that we might invalidate the land sale entirely. That ought to set them spinning!'

'So offhand, you'd estimate that perhaps three or four hundred people could be out to get you, Miss Anderson?' The lieutenant sounded just the slightest bit sarcastic.

Such numbers had never occurred to her. All she had dreamed of in her quest for vengeance was a single faceless creature who could be blamed for everything—

and perhaps run out of town on a rail! 'Good lord!' She looked up at Joel for support. He was nodding.

'People who might go to gaol tend to get pretty aroused,' the lieutenant continued. 'But people who might lose their property, they're the ones likely to blow their stacks—and yours!'

'I—good lord!' Speechless, Kitty shuddered.

'And then read this note,' said Joel. The paper was crumpled, dirty, covered with the red dust of the brick around which it had been wrapped. 'Get Out of Town,' it said, in letters printed apparently with a blue crayon. Kitty felt a sudden churning sickness in her stomach.

'Do they hate me that much?' she faltered.

'You hate *them*, don't you?'

'Yes, I guess I do. Although I ordinarily think of it as him, not them. My brother's life has been ruined, my career has been completely interrupted, I almost darn lost the family farm! What would you expect me to feel? Turn the other cheek, maybe? I guess I'm not that good a Christian.' A moment's pause, and then between stiff lips, 'I don't feel I have any reason to feel sorry for *them*, not a single one.'

'Well, that's entirely up to you, Miss Anderson.' Lieutenant Frankel examined the stalk he was chewing and threw it away. 'Provided maintaining your ideas doesn't break the law, that is. You mean to press on with your suit?'

'Of course I do!' Indignation was her strongest suit at the moment, and she pressed it.

'Then I suppose I'll have to take some action.' Lieutenant Frankel scrambled awkwardly to his feet. 'You'll be at the Carmody house for a time?'

Joel answered for her. 'For another week or ten days, at the very least.' The lieutenant walked long-leggedly over to the truck and climbed in. Joel came to face her, resting his hands on her shoulders. 'Don't let it frighten

you,' he murmured. 'There are lots of people around
these parts who love you.' He dropped a gentle kiss on
her forehead. 'Give you a ride back to the house?' he
asked. Kitty waved him off and then watched as the two
men drove back up the spine of the ridge.

She turned to take one more look at the water. The
sea was calm, sparkling calm, as the afternoon sun
painted a silver path across it. On the river one of the
small inshore fishing-boats was making for home, distance making its dingy grey look white, its tattered ensign
whole and beautiful. But the spirit had gone out of the
day, as always happened when reality intruded on
fantasy. Kit shrugged and started walking up the path
herself. Honey, the huge mastiff, noted her movements
and circled around to join up with her, giving up his
mastiff-dream of a thousand gulls destroyed. Everyone
hates you; somebody loves you! The first thought shook
her to the core; the second sustained her spirits. The birds
screamed and harried them all the way home.

The house seemed empty when she came in. No more
ringing the bell for the butler; now she came and went
as one of the family might. A pot-and-pan noise from
the kitchen attracted her attention, and she wandered
down to the swinging door under the stairs and poked
her head in. Mrs Wright was a great deal of cook, both
in size and in accomplishment, but not one to take
quickly to strangers. After sniffing around at each other
for three days she was almost on the point of accepting
Kitty.

'Miss Anderson?' She smiled. 'Come and set a spell?'

'Don't mind if I do—but please call me Kitty.
Everyone gone out?'

'No. Mr Carmody went off with Mary. His brother is
in the library. John's wife seems to have disappeared—

more good works, I suppose. She's chairwoman of so many things that I can't keep track. Have a lemonade?'

'Have you known the family long—Sara?' That had been the breaking point. 'Sara without the h,' the cook had explained only the day before. 'Not Sarah! You can hear the difference, can't you?'

And Kitty, who couldn't tell a penny's worth of difference between them, nodded agreement.

'Been with the Carmodys for—oh, nigh on to twenty years,' Sara admitted, then added a coy, 'Of course I started very young.'

'Of course. How about John? I don't understand him. He seems like a man who has all the world's troubles on his back, but I never see him actually *do* anything.'

'Yes, well . . .' the heavy arms were busy rolling dough for pies—homemade blueberry '. . .John was the second child, you know. There's always trouble for a second child. Joel was the oldest, the hardest worker. Frank— the one who died—was the most lovable—and then there was John. Who seemed to have been born with two left hands, if you get my drift.'

'Yes, I see. And then?'

'Well, when Joel had that terrible fight with his father and left the business, that put John on top for the first time in his life. He ran the corporation into the ground, until finally the stockholders begged Joel to come back. Just a couple of months ago, that is. Joel hated to get back into groceries; he had his own business, you know, doing right well down South some place. Taste that. Sweet enough?'

The pie-pans had been lined, and she was offering a spoonful of the blueberries as a sample.

'Lovely. Just right.' And a pause for appreciation. 'No, I didn't know he'd been out of the family business. I thought he was just in the grocery business.'

'Among other things,' chuckled Sara. 'Roamed the world, served in the military for a time, wrote adventure stories—— Lord, there isn't anything that Joel hasn't done.'

'Including taking care of babies?' Kitty threw it in casually, but the reaction was overwhelming.

'Huh!' Sara stopped and blew out a great breath of air. 'That—Jessica! Wouldn't lend a hand, not a minute's worth, to help with the baby. A sweet little thing she is too, the baby.' The conversation faded away to a mutter while Sara banged a couple of pans which didn't require the service.

'But you wouldn't mind taking the child on?' queried Kitty.

'Me? Of course I wouldn't—only Joel has this thing about family. The child must be loved by her own people, he says, not by hired hands! Some morning I suspect I'll come up to the house and find that woman murdered by her own brother-in-law!'

'You don't mean that!'

'Of course I don't, but—he needs help, Joel does. Spends all his time helping others, and needs it himself.' Which was the obvious beginning of a sermon that Kitty didn't wish to hear. She snatched a couple of chocolate-chip cookies from the jar and fled down the hall.

John was still in the library, singing softly. Kitty, attracted, skidded to a halt by the door and peered in. Joel's brother was sitting in an easy-chair, a brandy glass in his hand. He peered at her, grinned, and waved her an invitation to join him. Kitty sighed a truly feminine sigh. All those good looks, going to hell in a hand-basket! What a waste.

'Drink?' offered John.

'Orange juice. I'll get it,' she returned. 'Pills, you know.'

He nodded as if he understood. She took the chair opposite him and sank into it with a sigh. 'I've been walking, all the way down to the tip of the Neck. You seem happy?'

'Change of venue,' he said. 'They're holding the investigation now, so all I have to do is sit at home and wait. Wonderful relaxation.' He waved a hand vaguely at the stacks of books. 'I never was cut out to be a grocery clerk.' He nodded again, squinted one eye at her, and sat back. 'Married, are you? I can't remember your name.'

'Kitty, they call me. Actually it's Katherine. And no, I'm not married.'

'Good.' He took a sip from his glass and twirled the bulbous container until the remaining brandy almost spilled over the rim. 'Katherine—nice name. Good. Don't get married. Used to be my own boss, did you know that?' Kitty made adequate noises—not quite words, but close enough to satisfy him. 'Used to be my own boss. Could have licked all the problems. But that witch—she had to—damn. And then Joel came. Didn't used to drink before, did you know that?'

Kitty made a couple more throat-noises.

'Don't ever get married. Listen—damn women twist you around and tie you up in knots—they——' He stopped, fumbling for words.

'Drive you to drink?' she offered.

'Good lord, that's it,' he mumbled. 'You're a wise little witch. Smarter than they think! Maybe you'll fool them yet!' At which he swivelled his chair to look out of the window, and pointedly ignored her. Kitty stood guard for a moment or two, but there was to be no resumption of the conversation *that* afternoon!

And here I am, she told herself, right in the middle of the enemy camp, and—what was it that Faith had said? Find all his secrets hidden behind his socks? A stupid idea, but then the house was empty, the chance was here, and if she *didn't* look she'd be forever doubting!

She had a little trouble suppressing a giggle as she made her way slowly up the stairs, rejuvenated. Joel's room was at the end of the south wing, next to the nursery, where work had finally finished and Mary had been moved. Kitty stopped for a second to look around behind her, then opened the door and walked in. She had expected luxury; she got comfort. A real man's room, with a few heavy pieces of furniture, a thick brown rug, simple curtains at the windows, and—sure enough—a heavy chest of drawers with a mirror balanced on top.

There was no sign hung that said 'Spy socks in here,' so she fumbled through the top three drawers, fighting her way through T-shirts and jockey shorts and acres of handkerchiefs. Either Joel had a perpetually drippy nose, or he dated lots of women who cried! The thought came casually, and left her with a queer feeling of unexplainable emptiness. She pounded her tiny fist on the highly polished top of the chest, and only succeeded in aggravating her problem. Concentrate, she shouted inside her head. Concentrate!

When she knelt to the fourth drawer she found socks. All kinds of socks. Knee-socks, ankle-socks, plain black, plain grey, brilliant red—a rainbow of socks, all tidily rolled up in balls, each sock carefully tucked into its partner. There were enough there for a man with the normal two feet to change every day for a month! Kitty, who owned six pairs herself, gasped.

But you're here to spy, she lectured herself, and her hands began to fumble around among the piles of wool and cotton. The spying proved easier than anticipated. In the back of the drawer, under the pile of black socks, she came across a large manila envelope. Her immediate impulse was to cut and run. Instead she disciplined herself and forced her hands to pull the packet out into the open. The envelope was stuffed. Across the top was the imprint, 'Whaling City Investigations'. Written carelessly in pencil across one of the corners were the words 'Hopkins Neck'.

'Oh God!' Kitty muttered.

'Do you think He can help?' The voice was right at her ear, deep, masculine. Kitty came up with a stifled scream. The envelope fell to the floor, its contents scattered around the room. The top of her head slammed into Joel's jaw. He grabbed at her, whether to steady himself or to hold her in place she never knew. 'All right,' he soothed. 'All right, now.'

Thoroughly enfolded in his strong arms, pressed against his soft cotton shirt, she began to feel, after a moment, that perhaps it *might* be all right. The scream was demoted to mere mutterings and sobs. After a little back-patting the sobs were swallowed.

'So I've finally gotten you alone in my bedroom,' he murmured. His mouth was at her ear; she heard the words, felt the trembling gust of his warm breath, and felt fear edging her again—a different fear.

'No!' she gasped. Her feeble strength could hardly move his arm.

'No?' Joel chuckled, and moved her an inch or two away so he could see her dark eyes. 'How do you know for sure?'

'I—I know.' She was fighting a losing battle, and she knew it. Not that she might not have wriggled free, despite the strength of him. The problem was that her own muscle and mind didn't *want* her to escape. For a moment she fluttered at him like a trapped bird, beating at him ineffectually with her wings. And then all her opposition collapsed, and she hung in his arms without strength of her own.

'Lovely little Katherine,' he murmured, his mouth at her ear, nibbling. Kitty barely mustered a sigh. His mouth slipped, trailing kisses down from her ear, along her neck to her chin, and then up to where her lips waited, trembling. First contact was light, pleasant, swift. And then he came back to the assault, his lips warm and moist and altogether pleasant to taste. Comfort—a moment of comfort. And then, as he increased the pressure slightly, she felt an erotic pull that originated in her stomach and chased itself up her spine like the Charge of the Light Brigade. And just as suddenly she was no longer being kissed—she was kissing.

Her hands fumbled their way clear of his arms and made their way up around his neck, as she rose on the tips of her toes. Holding on for dear life, doing her best to squirm into him, she lost all her control over life, and became a mad excited thing, clinging around his neck and breathing hard during the intervals.

For a moment Joel stopped, held her off. 'No?' His eyebrows were raised in pseudo-astonishment. She felt the fierce need to follow this trail to its end.

'Shut up,' she muttered, and returned to her work. Time seemed to expand and then contract. In one second she was clinging to him on tiptoe. In the next she was stretched out on the bed, her blouse long since discarded, and he was lying beside her. One of his hands was resting on her naked stomach, just over her navel, while he drew erotic circles there. The other, in slow motion, was making a leisurely climb of her breast, striving towards the bronze peak which had so suddenly come erect. When his head came down to replace the venturesome hand she was startled for a moment, and waited, shivering with excitement, for what was to come. She could feel his tongue as it gently caressed that peak, then his lips touched gently.

'Oh lord!' she moaned as her body writhed without instructions. His head came up as he searched her face, then returned to its work. The hand over her navel stopped its senseless circling and moved down to struggle with the snaps on her trousers. The barrier held but for a moment, then fell to gentle persuasion. And his hand invaded the gap.

Somehow, in all that excitement they had squirmed around a quarter turn until Kitty's head hung out over the bed. Her hair had fallen down completely behind her, and almost touched the floor. Her body was covered with perspiration, her mind filled with violent and excruciating pleasure, when a little voice in her ear said rather loudly, 'Nuncle Joe?' and a squeal of displeasure accompanied it.

Kitty came down to earth with a massive thump. She was suddenly cold, as if someone had opened a refrigerator door in her face. And very far away, almost inaudible because of distance, she heard Joel mutter, 'Great day in the morning!' Which was just the way Kitty felt. She closed her eyes and prayed. Please let it all be in my imagination, Lord, she prayed. It isn't real, is it, God? You wouldn't let that little—child interrupt at a time like this?

The voice at her ear said 'Mama?' And the curtain came down on Kitty Anderson's great adventure. Came smashing down. The bed shook as Joel slid over the other side, did something to his clothes, and came around the bed. Little Mary turned to face the other way, watching her uncle. Kitty rolled over on to her stomach, struggled to re-button her trousers, then looked vainly for her blouse. The two Carmodys were having a conversation at two-year-old level, and as they talked her blouse came flying high in the air, above the child's field of view, and landed on top of her head.

Cautiously, Kitty slid herself away, across the mattress, and on to the floor on the far side, struggling to get into her blouse. One arm of the garment refused to co-operate. She had no idea where her bra had disappeared to—or when, for that matter. With one mighty push she forced her arm into the sleeve, ignoring the tearing sound along the seam. Fumbling fingers made the buttons fit, not necessarily in the right holes. She climbed up off her knees, and tried a step.

'Stay right where you are,' said Joel. He was smiling for Mary's benefit, but Kitty could hardly miss the cold steel aimed in her direction. She sat back down on the edge of the bed.

He picked up the baby, tossed her up a couple of times, and headed for the stairs. 'Mrs Wright,' he explained as he disappeared.

'And if you think I'm going to wait right here so you can come back and kill me, you've got another think coming,' muttered Kitty, taking some care not to be loud enough for him to hear. She came up off the bed, tucked her blouse into the waistband of her trousers, made a futile effort to tidy herself, and made for the door.

She might have made it too, but for two small problems. Her foot landed on one of those discarded pieces of paper, and she came to a hurried landing on her most prominent portion, right in the middle of the pile. The landing smarted; she blinked to control the tears, then her hand fell on one of the papers, and curiosity killed another of her nine lives. She was still reading when Joel came back, running up the stairs two at a time. He slammed the door behind him and stood with his back to it, glaring down at her.

'Now then, young lady?' She looked up at him, knuckling one eye to catch a recalcitrant tear. He expects some explanation from me? she thought wildly. The nerve of the man! It might be fun to be his wife. I could poison him slowly, over a lot of years, and laugh all the time!

'Well?'

Kitty took a deep breath and squirmed around facing directly towards him. 'I'm willing to hear your apology,' she said in a determined voice.

'*You're* ready to hear *my*—what colossal nerve! Why should I apologise? You're the one who sneaked into my room and——'

'I don't sneak,' she interrupted. 'And you tried to rape me. Here I am, practically an invalid in your care, and what do you do? You try to—to—well, you *did*!'

Joel folded his arms across his chest and glared. If looks could kill, Kitty would have lost her ninth life already. 'Listen,' he said, very coldly, very softly. 'I did *not* try to rape you. I seem to remember that you were helping all the way, whatever it was I was trying to do!'

'Seduction, then,' she muttered miserably. 'And I was certainly not trying to help you! You distinctly heard me say "no" at the very beginning. Admit it!'

He shrugged. 'So all right, you said "No" at the very beginning. It was a very weak no. And then you changed your mind!'

'I did no such thing!' she yelled at him, waving both hands—and the papers—in his direction. 'I *never* change my mind, just like I *never* get excited! Never!' Never get excited? Dr Meadows' warning came slamming into her mind, breaking past the anger-barrier she had been building. It cut all the courage out of her. She slumped down and really began to cry.

'Kit?' He was at her side, with one arm around her shoulders. She shook it off and cried harder. 'Katherine?' A nervous pause. 'That's not fair, Katherine.'

'What isn't?' She brushed her hair back out of her face, but the tears were still falling.

'Crying. That's a cheap trick, Katherine.'

'What do you expect? Cheers? A medal? I'm tired—exhausted. I don't feel well, you've scared me half to death, and I just want to go to bed—my own bed,' she hastened to add. 'Alone!'

'All right, I've got the message. Can you walk?'

'Of course I can walk.' She made the effort to stand up, managed to almost make it, then collapsed against him.

'I'm getting pretty good at catching you,' he noted glumly. 'You'd think we could build a relationship on a talent like that? I'd better carry you down the hall.' Kitty made no objection. The tears were under control, both her hands were filled with copies of reports, and Joel, as gloomy as a dark cloud, had failed to notice. When he stretched her out on her own bed she slipped her hands and the papers under her body.

'You want me to undress you?' he asked.

'Never,' she said. 'I'd hate that!'

'You didn't hate it the last time I did it,' he reasoned.

'If I'd known I would have hated it.' She gave him her most prim look. 'You can leave me now. Close the door as you go out.'

'Yeah,' he sighed, 'Close the door.' He did. From the outside. Kitty pulled herself up against her pillows, shut the tears off, and considered. 'If you'd closed that *other* door when you had the chance we wouldn't have been interrupted,' she murmured, disgusted with herself, and with life in general, but mostly with the inopportune Mary Carmody. The door came open again. Kitty almost jumped out of her skin, sliding down under the sheets just in case Joel had heard her last statement.

'I'll bring your dinner up,' he said, and was gone. Kitty came back up out of the sheets and swung her feet out on to the floor. Lying down had become a dangerous occupation, one that she wanted to avoid for a time while she thought things over.

So you need to balance the good and the bad, the lucky and the unlucky, she lectured herself. First of all, you were *lucky* that he left his bedroom door open, and even more lucky that the baby wandered in. If ever there was a woman about to give everything up in response to pure sexual impulse—lust—you were it, kiddo. Lust is the better word for it. A nasty word! Stick to that. Whatever happened to 'keep myself pure for my wedding night'? Out the window, huh! And he didn't have to apply any great pressure, did he? Katherine Anderson! You must have been born with round heels. All he had to do was push just the tiniest bit! So you're lucky that little Mary wandered in. Remind yourself tomorrow to give the kid a big kiss! Or maybe she'd prefer chocolate ice-cream?

Next subject. Whatever happened to Sir Lancelot? At the very first opportunity, at a time when you were tired and—ill—how about that, he purposefully took advantage of your convalescent state! That's a black mark on his slate. Come to think of it, wasn't that what happened to King Arthur and his bride? And then he purposefully took advantage of your loss—temporary loss—of inhibitions. That's another black mark on him! You could, Katherine, just by a little judicious evaluation of the subject from a different angle, recognise that it was all *his* fault from beginning to end!

And you, Kitty—you're not really responsible for what happened! You're as pure as the driven snow, love, and he's as black a villain as ever came out of Hollywood. Right? Right!

Having thought herself to a convoluted but more acceptable estimate of the scene, Kitty put her hands behind her and leaned back on the bed. The rattle of paper surprised her. She had forgotten the papers! She whirled around and almost dived under the sheets to rescue whatever documents she could find. Four sheets of paper remained.

But only a fool repeated past mistakes. Filled with new energy, Kitty bounced off the bed and headed for the door. For a second she fiddled with the simple bolt, only to be stopped by another thought. Had Joel gone back to his own room? If so, did he pick up all the papers and hide them away some place?

For girls of Kitty's nature, thought immediately brought action. Instead of locking her door she eased it open a hair, just enough so that she could see down the long narrow hall. Nothing moved. She opened the door another inch or two, and was just about to squeeze out when she heard voices. Her door closed gently. Not to the full extent of its latch, but far enough to *look* closed, but still have a narrow crack open. John was striding down the hall, lashed on by his wife Jessica's acid tongue.

'You're a fool, John,' the lady was saying, perhaps for the tenth time. 'You were sitting there drinking with that Anderson woman? What did you say——? Oh, don't bother, I'm sure you're too drunk to remember.'

'I remember,' rumbled John. 'Nice kid. Smarter than you think.'

'And you'd just better remember *that*,' Jessica snapped. 'That girl is dangerous, and don't you forget it!'

'I won't.'

'And you're off the bottle just as long as that—person—is in our house.'

'Off? Not on your orders, lady. I've already decided to give it up. Joel's right, I need to assert myself around here more.'

'That'll be the day!' His wife had finally guided him to their bedroom door, two down from Kitty's room. 'You just keep your nose out of things, John Carmody, or some of my friends will come and break your legs. Do you understand that?'

Evidently John did. Kitty heard no more noises, and their door slammed behind them as she shut her own door and wandered back to the bed. No, she told herself, this isn't the time to go around playing spy. 'My friends will break your legs!' Good lord, what have they gotten themselves into? And what have I gotten *myself* into? She collapsed on the bed. Sometimes, she admitted, it becomes very hard for a girl who's all mush inside to pretend she's a strong, aggressive character. For a girl like me. All of which brought more tears, which were still running when a brief knock sounded on the door, and Joel came in backwards, carrying a tray.

'I brought your dinner,' he said jovially.

'Thank you,' she burbled through her tears.

'Great day, are you still crying?' he demanded.

'A girl's allowed to cry when she wants to. Who appointed you to be chief censor?'

'Hey, don't growl at me! I wouldn't interfere with your God-given rights. Cry away. Only Mrs Wright says the soup is very thin. If you're going to cry into it, it will only make things worse!'

Kitty brushed her hair aside, sniffed up a remaining tear, and searched the room for a tissue. There was a box by her bed. Joel set the tray down on the side table and fetched her one. 'Blow your nose. You'll feel better.'

'I'll never feel better,' she snapped. 'Stop trying to cheer me up! I don't *want* to be cheered.' But she complied with the instructions anyway, and, strangely enough, did feel better. And after eating the entire meal, and trying her best not to smile at his terrible puns, she felt very much better indeed.

So, along about eleven o'clock, when she finally convinced him that it was past her bedtime, he came over to the bed and became serious for a moment. 'I owe you an apology, Kit. This afternoon's fiasco shouldn't have happened. I was so swept up in——'

'Lust.' He was fishing for a polite word, so she furnished the one that fitted.

'Well——' he refused to take it up '—I completely forgot how ill you'd been, how little time you've had to recover. I *do* apologise.'

It's nice to have him on the hip, Kitty thought as she studied every inch of his craggy face. Sincerity never shone so strongly. But be a little sceptical, she warned herself. Apologies are often just words strung together. 'And you'll never ever do that again?' she prompted.

'Oh, lord, no. I couldn't promise *that*!' The twinkle was back in his green eyes again, and both sides of his mouth curled up without actually smiling. 'A man would have to be insane to promise something so stupid. You're a beautiful woman, Katherine. I don't propose that I'm going to jump on you every time you come down the hall—but on the other hand, I wouldn't rule it out either. Goodnight, sexpot.'

He bent over to kiss her on her cheek, but she was so busy manoeuvring out of his way that the kiss landed full on her lips, gave her spirits a jump-start, and when he walked out of the door, whistling, she sat back against the pillows, a bemused smile on her face.

Some fifteen minutes later she had managed to break out of her dream-world. That world had turned to gold, an unusual condition for the town grouch to be in, she told herself, and her wandering hand fell on the papers she had stolen from his bedroom.

Papers, she told herself, and picked them up. At first her eyes refused to focus, but when they finally did so the shock brought her back to normality.

Each of the four sheets was a separate report. Joel Carmody was having someone followed. And each paper was a report of one day's activity of Francis Randolph.

Kitty ran the name through her mental file a couple of times before she found it. Francis Randolph, the only son of that Mr Randolph at the bank. The only son of that Mr Randolph, the selectman. Why would Joel want to know what Francis Randolph was up to? She did not find the answer to that question. The surveillance reports only indicated where the man went, when he met someone, how long they were together, and who the other person was.

Kitty raced through the first two sheets, then went over them again. Several names were included on each sheet. Of course, she told herself, he's bound to meet a good many people in the course of the day. But one name came up in both reports. Harris—the man from the subdivision. Kitty's eyes blinked and went out of focus. She was too tired to examine further, too tired to think. The other papers must wait for another day. It was a very sober young lady who tucked them into the drawer of her bedside table much later that night. A young lady who found it impossible to sleep during the hours of darkness, but who finally dropped off just as the sun came up over the edge of the Atlantic Ocean and sent its fingers prying into the world of Northport again.

CHAPTER SIX

KITTY dressed and came down to breakfast shortly after nine o'clock. Although she had spent a restless night her built-in clock refused to let her lie abed. The breakfast nook was next to the kitchen; a tiny room with a round table that could seat six, and then space for two massive sideboards, one on either side.

Jessica was sitting alone at the table, still in her nightgown, but wearing over it a lacy creation of blue and gold that served as a robe. Kitty fingered her worn trousers, her faded yellow blouse, and felt just a little out of place. 'Good morning,' she offered tentatively.

Jessica looked up. Without her make-up she was a pale imitation of the beauty of the previous night. Her thin face looked worn. There were more than a few crow's feet at the corner of her eyes. Her trim figure looked as if its foundation had collapsed. But she was more human. 'Good morning——'

'Kitty.'

'Yes, of course, forgive me. I'm not at my best in the morning. Good morning, Kitty. Just stick your head around the door and tell Mrs Wright what you want for breakfast.' Kitty complied, then came back, served herself a mug of coffee from the sideboard, and sat down. Jessica folded up her morning copy of the *Globe* and set it aside.

'A bad habit,' she said. 'Reading newspapers at the table. I have to keep up with the financial section, and there's hardly time in the day. And then again, of course,

107

there's seldom anyone to share breakfast with me, you know.'

'Oh, I didn't realise,' Kitty apologised. 'I thought you did things with charities and good works and things like that.'

'That too,' Jessica laughed. There was a shrill quality about that laugh, as if she were a woman under great strain. 'But in addition, I also serve as treasurer of the Family corporation.'

And there it is again, Kitty thought. The Family corporation, with a capital F, almost as if it were some religion that required a daily sacrifice and choral.

'Mr Carmody?' Kitty hesitated to call him John. 'He doesn't come down for breakfast?'

'He never gets out of bed before noon.'

'Joel and Mary? They certainly never sleep late. At least the baby doesn't, does she?'

Jessica made a little face, then laughed. 'Oh, they've gone long since. We never know what Joel's up to, he's been away so long. In fact I first met him at our wedding, and from then till two weeks ago he's been a stranger. A curious family, the Carmodys.'

Kitty sipped at her coffee, then set the mug down. 'Yes, I can see that. Although—I mean, I've only known Joel——'

'Isn't that strange?' Jessica made a vague stab at the sausage on her plate, then gave up in favour of a crumpled corner of a roll. 'Here we've lived for the past five years—well, during the winters, I mean. We usually go to Bermuda for the summer. And we've never met you. Not once.'

'I've been away,' Kitty told her. 'Military service first, then a speed-up education in advanced computer techniques, and a job—until a year ago when my brother got into so much trouble.' Another sip at the coffee. Your business is getting information, not giving it, she reminded herself. Ask, don't answer! 'Joel and John, they seem so—different from each other.'

'Different mothers,' said Jessica, reflecting. 'Joel's mother walked out on the old man. John's mother wished she could, but never did. She died when he was six years old.'

Sara Wright interrupted at that moment, bearing a plate of scrambled eggs and a double serving of toast. 'Oh, I couldn't possibly eat that much!' Kitty complained.

'Orders,' said Sara, smiling. 'The boss said you're too thin, and I should feed you up.'

'He's not *my* boss,' Kitty snapped. 'And I don't think I want to be fed like some prize brood mare!'

'Hear, hear!' Jessica applauded. 'Behold a free spirit!' Sara went back into the kitchen, muttering. 'You almost sound as if you don't like Joel?'

It was a question with barbs on it. Kitty, through a long sleepless night, had finally concluded that she liked Joel Carmody very much indeed, fair weather or foul! But that was something one just didn't blurt out at the breakfast table. That was a conclusion that one savoured, tasted, cherished to oneself. Upset, but striving to keep a straight face, she managed to stammer, 'I—do you?'

Jessica thought about it for a moment, a slow smile building on her face. 'That's a hard question to answer,' she said at last. 'To be honest, if I'd met Joel before I met John— well! John is the good-looking one, but Joel has what it takes.'

'Has what it takes for what?'

Jessica burst out laughing, setting her cup back into its saucer. 'Can you really be so naïve, my dear?' Kitty could feel the blush running up into her cheeks.

'No, of course not,' she mumbled, turning her attention to her plate.

There was a conversational lull. Kitty, with her head down, paying strict attention to her meal, missed the series of expressions that succeeded each other on Jessica Carmody's face. The last one to appear was certainly— satisfaction.

'You know,' Mrs Carmody said, 'you mustn't take Joel too much for granted. He's a man with a world full of experience with women. I'm afraid, Kitty, that I can see you falling in love with someone like Joel. It would be a terrible danger to you. He's much older than you. By a good ten years, I suspect. He's thirty-one.' Only six years older, Kitty told herself. Not too old at all!

'And the *kinds* of experience he's had, you wouldn't want to know. He eats little girls like you, Kitty.'

'Yes, I've noticed his big teeth,' Kitty responded glumly. 'Doesn't he have any *good* traits?'

'Not so I've noticed.' Jessica pushed her chair back. 'You'll have to excuse me now. I have to do a million things, and I have an important lunch meeting today.'

'Of course. Thank you for your advice.'

Jessica got up from the table, paused as if she were going to say something else and then changed her mind. After the door had closed behind her Sara came in with a fresh pot of coffee, and topped up Kitty's mug.

'Don't pay too much attention to advice given around this house,' the cook warned. 'Eat up. If you don't I'll lose my job when word gets back to Himself.'

'Himself?' queried Kitty.

'The big man. The boss.'

'Are you afraid of Joel, Sara?'

'No, but you should be!' The cook grinned down at her, patted her shoulder, did an imitation wolf-howl, and disappeared into the kitchen, laughing all the way. Kit shook her head and surveyed the table. 'Crazy,' she murmured. 'They're all crazy!'

*   *   *

Her lawyer came at about eleven o'clock. Only John remained at home, and, Sara said, 'He's buried himself in his books. He used to be a great scholar, you know. Now—well, you've seen.' Kitty was standing outside on the front lawn enjoying the sunshine when Faith Latimore drove up. The two mastiffs were frolicking around at her feet.

'Walking the dogs? I thought you hated dogs.' Faith rolled down the window of her car, but did not get out.

'I don't exactly *hate* dogs,' Kitty replied. 'For some reason these stupid beasts think I'm a nice person, and who am I to disabuse them?'

'Who indeed? Look, I only have a minute. The town administrator came through in fine style, much to my surprise. I think *he* thinks there's something phoney going on in the Public Works Department. Here are copies of all the perk tests. I've given a set to our investigator, there's a set for myself, and a set for you. Go through them in your spare time——'

'That's all I've got, is spare time,' mourned Kitty. But Faith was no source of sympathy.

'Good,' she said as she handed over the envelope. 'Then you can expend a considerable amount on these things.'

'But what do I look for?'

'Inconsistencies. Anything even the least bit out of the ordinary. I can smell the orange-blossom way out here. When's the wedding?'

'Wedding?' Kitty gasped, and all the colour ran out of her face. 'What are you talking about?'

'The wedding,' said Faith, laughing. 'If I were you I wouldn't settle for anything less than a wedding. Well, maybe I would at that! He's some handsome hunk! G'bye.' Kitty was left with a handful of paper and hair full of wind as the lawyer gunned the car in a circle and headed back towards town.

Good lord, she thought, it's not only the Carmodys who've lost their marbles! Wedding! What an odd thought. Why don't you think about weddings, Katherine? Because they scare you? Because *he* scares you? Or are you just all a-tremble because you might have to give up the tiniest corner of that hard-nosed independence you've treasured so long?

She might well have driven herself to distraction, but Honey, the elder of the two dogs, came over at just that moment and sniffed at her. 'I can't help it if even my friends are a bit strange,' Kitty told him. He panted, seeming to understand. 'And now *I've* got papers to hide,' she explained to the animal. 'Should I take them in and hide them behind my socks?' The dog offered one sharp bark. 'No, I agree with you. I know, I'll take them down to my own house and look them over. Plenty of privacy. Care to come along for the walk?' The dog fell in at her side.

Kitty knew she was healthier, just by the shortness of the walk. She bounced down the path to the brook in a matter of minutes, dabbled in the coolness of the pool, and went on to the house. There seemed to be an aura of happiness surrounding her world, and she wasn't prepared to challenge the feeling. Her spare key was under the doormat, where every other country family kept theirs. She was busy explaining all this to Honey as she unlocked the door and walked across the threshold. The dog brushed by her and growled. 'Oh, my!' Kitty exclaimed.

What once had been a relatively neat little room was now a vandalised mess. All the furniture had been overturned. The rug had been torn up, gathered, and was piled in a far corner. All the papers in and on her desk were scattered, all her business records, all her personal notes. The pictures on the wall had been removed and smashed. In a state of shock Kitty moved across the room and picked up the photograph of her father and mother. The glass was gone, the picture crumpled. She held the ruin against her breast. The dog growled.

Had it not been for that growl Kitty might have spent a lifetime in her haunted dreams. The dog brought her back to reality. People who vandalised houses did it for some purpose. And they might well stay around to ruin more than the house! Kitty backed up towards the front door, still clutching the photograph in both hands. Fear chased up and down her spine—fear and hatred. For more than a year she had gathered up a hatred aimed at some unspecified person, but it was a one-way sort of emotion. She hated.

A few days earlier, with the visit of Lieutenant Frankel, she had felt the first time a touch of fear from those who hated *her*. It had been an uncomfortable feeling; and now her house lay before her as an example. People *did* hate her. For a dozen reasons, she supposed. But they did exist!

She backed a few steps further away until she bumped into the bole of the apple tree just outside the front door. From inside the house she could hear the continued growls as the mastiff searched. Whoever had done the damage had fled; Honey appeared at the door without giving further alarm, and wandered over to sit by her feet. She dropped one hand and felt the sudden cold as the big dog licked her fingers.

It was a hot summer day; Kitty felt cold shivers as she retreated up the hill towards the trees and the lively brook. The armour of her own one-way crusade had been pierced. Where vengeance had sustained her for almost a year, now the sword was reversed, the point close to her own heart. She slumped down on one of the granite boulders beside the pool and closed her eyes, suddenly afraid of the world around her.

'So this is where you've been hiding!' A warm sincere voice, full of sympathy. Kitty opened both eyes; Joel was standing in front of her, with both hands extended in her direction.

The papers in her hands—the perk test results, the photograph of her parents, all scattered in the winds as she seized his extended hands and was pulled up into the warmth and safety of him. 'Thank God!' she sobbed, as the tears began to fall.

'Try some more of this,' Joel offered as he handed her a container. Without looking Kitty sipped. Orange juice. She swallowed and came back for more, holding the tiny plastic cup between both shaking hands. 'There now,' he comforted, 'it's all over.'

Kitty had cried herself dry. She polished off the orange juice and handed back the empty glass. 'I must look a fright,' she murmured.

His head leaned back and he bellowed with laughter. 'Typical woman!'

She managed a very plausible glare. 'A lot you know!'

'So tell me.' They were both sitting on the granite boulder. One of his strong arms was around her waist, the other hand, holding one of his huge handkerchiefs, was still dabbing at her eyes.

'You don't need to do that,' she mumbled. 'I'm through crying.'

Joel put the handkerchief away, and used the free arm to wrap her up completely. It was comforting, inside the little nest he created for her. Kitty relaxed, let her ear rest against his chest, heard the steady thunder of his strong heart. 'Not too warm?'

'No. I've been cold—oh, Joel, why do people——?' She buried her face again, unable to say more.

He coaxed her, 'Why do people do what?' His fingers trailed gently through her hair, undoing all the braiding, letting it fly in the winds like a flag.

'Why do people hate?'

He pushed her an inch or two away and tilted her chin upward with one finger. '*You* ask *me* that, Kitty? My, but we're changing, aren't we?'

She pushed him away, not really wanting to do so. 'Don't make fun of me,' she muttered. His arms pulled her back against his chest again.

'I won't.' The soothing hand was back in her hair again. 'Tell me about it.'

'Come and see.' His arms unfolded reluctantly. Kitty stood up, making minimal repairs as she did, straightening her trousers, re-buttoning the top of her blouse, brushing her hair back behind her ears. And then she took his hand and led him down the incline to the house. The front door was still half open. He pushed it back and smothered an oath.

The dog growled again as he walked across the threshold. 'The dog can smell him,' said Joel. 'Let's see what happens.' He took Honey's collar and led the mastiff out into the yard. 'Hunt!' he commanded.

The dog yipped and took a couple of steps towards the tree, circled, and came back again. The animal whined a couple of times as if following false leads, then it bayed and headed down the drive. Joel snatched at Kitty's hand and started to follow, but she objected.

'I don't want to see it,' she said stubbornly.

'See what?'

'I don't know. Whatever there is to see!'

'Then you'll stay here and wait?'

She shook her head so fiercely that her long blonde hair went flying. 'I—no, I don't want to be alone!'

'There's nothing to be afraid of. It's the middle of the afternoon on a bright sunny day, and there's not a soul in sight.'

'Yes, that's what bothers me. This didn't happen by itself—but there's not a soul in sight. All right, I'll—come with you.'

He took her hand again and led her gently down the driveway in the wake of the big dog. The animal had sniffed its way slowly down to the street, puzzled for a moment in the gutter, then set off at a more rapid pace for the housing development across the street. Joel lengthened his stride, towing Kitty behind him.

'Not so fast!' she gasped. 'I'm not all that speedy!'

He relented. The dog had slowed too, just outside one of the larger houses in the division. Two cars were parked in the carport beside the house. Windows and doors were closed. Out at the back an air-conditioner laboured. Children lived in the subdivision, but there was not one in sight. Besides themselves, only the swirling seagulls showed life. The dog made up its mind.

It turned into the drive of the big house and sniffed its way to the front door. Joel, still towing Kitty behind him, hurried up the walk and rang the bell. There was no answer.

'Nobody home,' Kitty suggested. Her teeth were beginning to chatter again. She moved closer to Joel. 'Why don't we——?'

'I saw the curtain move as we came up the walk,' he said grimly. His finger punched at the bell again, then rattled the decorative brass knocker. Footsteps sounded, slow-moving footsteps, and the door opened a chain's-worth.

'Yes?' A middle-aged woman, hair touched with grey, and a frightened expression on her face. 'I'm Mrs Harris. What do you want?'

'We want to talk to your husband,' said Joel. His voice was low and flat, threatening.

'He's—he's at work in the city.'

'If he is, he walked all the way,' Joel said. 'His car is parked over there under the carport. We don't intend to go away until we've seen him, Mrs Harris, so you might as well go and get him.'

Some moments later the door opened a little wider, and a man stood there. Bill Harris was one of the commuter set. As vice-president of a local bank in New Bedford he wore all the accoutrements of a successful businessman. About six feet tall, he appeared to weigh over two hundred pounds. His face was florid. 'If you people don't go away I'm going to call the police,' he told them.

'Fine. Fine,' Joel assured him. 'That'll save me the bother. But be sure you make it the State police, friend, because this is a criminal matter.' Harris swallowed hard and stepped back a pace. It was just enough for Honey to take advantage. The huge dog pushed by him and began sniffing across the floor.

'Invite us in,' Joel continued. 'You wouldn't want all the neighbours to hear, I suppose?'

Harris retreated another step, and made a movement that might possibly be construed as an invitation. Joel walked over the threshold, towing Kitty behind him. The dog had already turned right into a corridor, and was now sitting in front of a closed door, scratching. When Joel came up behind him Honey loosed a tremendous baying that shook the house to its foundations.

'Who do you suppose is in there?' Joel reached out for the knob.

'You can't go in there. That's my son's room!' Mrs Harris brushed by them all and stood between them and the door. Her hand was shaking, but she looked determined.

'Then why don't you ask your son to come out?' The steel was back in Joel's voice. Kitty, clinging for dear life to his hand, brushed up closer to him and wished she were at least a mile away.

'It doesn't take a lot of courage to vandalise the house of a little girl who can't protect herself,' Joel added. There was another moment of silence, and the door opened. The youth was a carbon copy of his father, perhaps an inch or two taller, and not so weighty. The minute the door started to open Honey had his nose in the gap, and when the door was completely opened the dog sniffed a couple of times at the young man and then sat down and stared at him.

'My son would never do anything like that,' Mrs Harris maintained. 'Junior's a good boy——'

'Who was in the Anderson kitchen,' Joel interrupted. 'If he didn't do it himself, he was there and saw who *did* do it. Want to tell us about it, son?'

The youth shook his head and refused to utter a word.

'Just a little boyish prank,' his father suggested. 'It could happen to anybody, you know. Just a——'

'Just a case of breaking and entering with intent,' Joel interrupted. 'Now, may we use your telephone? I'd like to call the police.'

'Please,' Mrs Harris interrupted nervously. 'He's a good boy. He—he's only eighteen, and planning to go into college in September, and a criminal conviction——'

'Shut up, Martha,' her husband interjected. 'Don't say another word!'

'No, your husband's right.' Joel grinned at them all, with that sort of wide-open smile that a shark uses before he bites. 'We'll prefer charges, of course. And in the meantime——'

Kitty watched, but could hardly believe what she saw. The Harris boy was inches taller than Joel; his father topped Joel by at least an inch and outweighed him by thirty pounds. But Joel reached with his right hand for the boy's shirt-front and lifted him up on to the tips of his toes, and with the other hand did exactly the same to the father. He pulled them both together in front of him and gave a good shake that rattled both their heads.

'Now hear this,' he almost whispered. 'The little lady is *not* alone. If I ever hear of anyone causing her any trouble for any reason, I'm going to come hunting for the pair of you.' One more shake to emphasise what he was saying. 'I don't care,' he continued, 'whether *you* cause any other incidents, or whether you're a hundred miles away. *Anybody* disturbs the peace and quiet of my little lady, and first I come for you. Is that clear?' To punctuate the paragraph he repeated the shakes after each of the last three words. And then he threw the pair of them away.

The father fell back on to a large sofa behind him. The son slammed into the wall and slid down, ending up sitting on the floor, his lower lip trembling. 'By the way,' Joel added in a conversational tone of voice, 'Honey here has a daughter. They'll both be roaming the farm across the street from now on. And they bite.'

He gave them all a cheerful smile, and began towing Kitty out towards the door, where another thought stopped him. 'Maybe prosecution isn't the thing,' he mused. 'It would be too bad for a kid your age to have a criminal record. I tell you what I'm going to do. I'm going to take Miss Anderson back up to my place for an hour or so.' He stopped to consult his wristwatch. 'That would make it about four o'clock. If, by four o'clock, when I come back down, the house across the street is all straightened up, cleaned and polished, I'll forget the charges—for just this one time.'

He ushered Kitty out of the door, nudged Honey until the dog got the message too, then looked back into the house. 'Thank you for your hospitality, Mrs Harris,' he called as he closed the door gently behind him. 'Close your mouth, Kitty,' he added with a chuckle as he towed her back up to the main road.

'I don't understand you,' Kitty told him for the hundredth time. They were back in the drawing-room of the Carmody house, each nursing a finger of brandy—for medicinal purposes, of course. Little Mary was playing in the middle of the room, being a mountain-climber, with Honey stretched out on his back, playing mountain.

'I don't understand me either,' Joel replied. 'Wasn't I brave?'

'Stop playing games with me!' Kitty stamped her little foot, to no avail; the rug had a three-inch nap. 'Your little lady, indeed!'

'Oh, that. I thought I might get away with *that*. Which part doesn't apply? Little? I bet you buy all your clothes in the girls' department!' It was so close to the truth that Kitty was thrown off guard. 'And you certainly *are* a lady!'

Only a day earlier Kitty would have argued that point too. Now she wasn't so sure she wanted to. Life had become more than a little bit upsetting.

'And my house?' Don't be too eager, her conscience dictated, but her tongue was out of control.

'All cleaned up.' Joel laughed as he swallowed the contents of his glass and poured himself another. 'The one thing I remember about your house, Kitty, was that nothing above five feet high ever seemed to get polished. You should see it now. Everything glistens all the way up to the ceiling! And oh, I forgot—here are those things you dropped by the pool.' He handed her the big envelope containing the perk tests, and then the picture of her father and mother.

'Nice-looking people,' he commented. 'Your parents?'

Kitty nodded, snatching at the photograph and hugging it.

'Old line Yankees?'

'You couldn't be further from the truth,' she replied. 'Immigrant stock from Sweden, both of them. My grandparents came over right after World War One. Land was cheap in those days. My dad poured every cent he could beg, borrow or steal into the farm.'

'What's in the envelope?'

Kitty, still playing 'who can you trust?' in a big hard world, shrugged. 'Just some papers from the business.' He grinned, but made no effort to push her.

'I've got to go back up to Boston tomorrow,' he offered. 'Why don't you give me that photograph and I'll have someone put a frame around it for you.'

'All in one day?'

'Why, of course. I'm a man of some importance.'

'Would you please stop teasing me, Joel? I can't decide whether you're the nicest man I ever met, or a consummate pig!'

'I'm telling nothing but the truth,' he insisted. 'I have character references. Ask Mary.'

At the sound of her name the baby tumbled over the dog, managed to get to her feet, and came running over to her uncle, babbling away.

'See? How's that for a reference? And if that won't do, just step into the kitchen and ask Sara Wright!'

'I don't have to ask Sara,' Kitty responded. 'She's told me more than I'd care to know about your wonderful character. In fact I think——'

Joel waited expectantly for the next word to drop. It never did. At long last Kitty had managed to put a stranglehold on her tongue. If he was *really* a nice guy, there was no use swelling his ego with comments like that! Sara Wright had spent the last two days acting as his sales agent, looking for a wife for the man!

He continued to ramble, but Kitty was so busy handling the one situation that clogged her mind, and as a result she got caught in the next. He was saying something while her mind was in turmoil, and she missed every word of it. In the dead silence that followed both Joel and Mary were staring at her.

'Will you?'

With no idea what he wanted, but too proud to display her ignorance, she smiled at them both and said, 'Of course I will.'

'Bless your little heart!' Within seconds she was picked up and whirled around him three full turns. 'I told you so, Mary,' he told the baby. 'You get to spend all day tomorrow with Kitty!'

By the time Kitty got to bed that night the little incident had grown into a major project. She hung up her clothes and slipped into her nightgown and slid under the sheets. The pillows lacked comfort. She sat up and punched them a time or two before resettling. No improvement. It's all in your mind, she told herself. You knew from day one that he wanted a temporary baby-sitter. You held out a long time, Katherine girl, but he finally got what he wanted, didn't he? Now tell me, what in the world do you do with a baby that young—for the entire day?

The thought bothered her so much that she finally got up and went over to her bureau, where the stack of papers waited. Evaluate them, Faith had said. 'But I don't have the slightest idea what to look for,' she muttered as she climbed back into bed and opened the envelopes. There were forty-eight test reports, one for each house in the subdivision. Their purpose was simple: to measure the capacity of each house-lot to absorb run-off from the cesspools used in the countryside in place of sewer connections.

And here they were. Each lot identified, all the figures entered, and she had no idea what the figures meant. At the bottom of each one was the approval stamp of the Department of Public Works. 'Approved for building,' it said, and there was a place for the date and the initials of the appropriate party.

So, if you don't know what the words mean, or how the numbers accrue, how can you evaluate? she thought. There was only one way she knew. See if the numbers added up. Not totally to her surprise some of them didn't, but the errors seemed too small to be of any importance. But there was something else. More than half of the separate lot-approvals had exactly the *same* figures! Kitty puzzled about that and found no useful answers. She was still reviewing lot number thirty-one when she fell asleep.

And had terrible dreams for the rest of the night. Kitty Anderson, chained to a rock, while all the townspeople went by, one at a time, and threw garbage at her, while Joel Carmody stood to one side with a big grin on his face and sold tickets!

CHAPTER SEVEN

KITTY came downstairs the next morning, riding Mary on her ample hip. The sun was hardly up. The whole world outside was in shadows. Mrs Wright was moving slowly around her domain. 'Don't perk up until after my third cup of coffee,' she reported as Kitty and the baby came through into the kitchen. 'I hear tell you've volunteered for hard labour?'

'Not exactly volunteering,' Kitty grumbled as she set the child down in her high-chair. It wasn't the time of day, but rather the manner of her awakening that upset her. Before she had even one eye open Joel had come waltzing into her bedroom singing some silly childish song, with Mary riding on his shoulder. 'Up, sleepyhead!' he sang. 'The day begins!'

'Go away,' Kitty muttered as she ducked under the sheets. 'Nobody gets up early and sings. Go soak your head!'

'No, no,' Joel replied. 'I'm on my way to Boston. Mary's had her fun, and now it's your turn.' At which point he deposited the baby on Kitty's stomach, wet nappy and all. Kitty squealed and was out of bed in a second, shaking her finger at him.

'Lovely,' he said, his eyes running up and down her long lawn cotton nightgown with the violets embroidered across the square yoke. 'Lovely. Every woman should have one——'

'What are you blathering about? It's a perfectly respectable nightgown!'

'Of course it is.' His laughter was infectious. 'Every woman should have one like that—to hang on your bedpost in case of fire. G'bye.'

And with that monstrous comment he ducked out of the door, just ahead of her swinging hand. Kitty was shaking as she turned back to the laughing child. Her anger cooled quickly, overborne by her real feelings for him. Every day should start like this, she told herself—then she noticed Mary's nappy. Well—almost every day.

She had taken another lesson the day before. It hardly required more than fifteen minutes for her to change the child. Of course there had been some minor variations. In place of the cloth nappies that Mary normally used, disposable ones had been substituted for the day. And now Kitty looked across the kitchen table, a little bleary-eyed, and said, 'But what can be so hard about watching a little kid for a day?'

'Never tried it, have you?' Sara poured her a cup of coffee, and barely managed to rescue the baby's food dish from being dumped on the floor.

'No,' Kitty admitted. 'But millions of people do it every day, so I figure I can.'

'Surprises me,' Mrs Wright allowed. 'When you first came you didn't like dogs; now Honey follows you around like you was his mother. Then you didn't like kids; now you volunteer to baby-sit?'

Kitty hid her face behind her coffee mug and sipped for courage. 'You don't have to be in love with kids to watch them,' she maintained. 'You don't have to like dogs to—well, I can't help it. The darn animal's done me a good turn or two, and—and he tricked me into it! That man!'

'No need to explain to me,' Sara Wright laughed as she filled Mary's plate with oatmeal. 'Want some?'

'Me? Oatmeal? Not a chance! That stuff's for——'

'Tut, tut,' Sara chuckled. 'Little ears!'

'I—you mean she understands what we're saying?'

'Of course she does. The kid's twenty-six months old, for goodness' sakes. Eat, Mary!'

The baby smiled at both of them, picked up her plastic spoon, and almost managed to get some oatmeal into her mouth. Kit sighed as she loaned a directional hand. The baby's milk was easier; it came in a sealed cup with a plastic cover and a drinking spout. Mary drank heartily, then, seemingly by accident, tossed the cup in the general direction of Honey, who was lying in the corner. The dog, more than willing to play, took the thin plastic container between his massive teeth, and there was milk all over the floor.

Only forty minutes later breakfast was over. Mary had some oatmeal in her stomach, somewhat more than that on her nose and cheeks and chin, all flavoured with a little of the orange juice which Kitty had judiciously guarded. Kitty herself had barely managed a piece of toast, a few sips of tepid coffee, and half a glass of fruit juice. And the child was indicating boredom.

'Time to change the subject,' Sara recommended. 'What did you plan?'

'Plan?' Kitty asked. 'You have to plan?'

'If you want to survive,' Sara said. 'Bath?'

'Why not? Bath, Mary?' The child agreed. Not waiting for any other encouragement, Kitty snatched her up under one arm, carried her own orange juice with her, and headed for the bathtub. The big mastiff, Honey, followed them out of curiosity.

How could bathing be a problem? Kitty hummed to herself as she undressed the child, tested the water and dunked her. Mary, all excitement, began to eat the soap-bubbles and splash water over the sides of the tub. Kit grabbed a towel and covered the floor protectively as she sat back on her heels. Not too shabby, she told herself.

Anybody can handle kids. That cracked sound coming from deep in her throat was a song; Kitty hadn't sung for months. Honey stretched out on the bath-towel, his great muzzle resting between his front paws.

So there, wise guy Carmody, Kitty chuckled. Thought I couldn't do it, huh? Thought I'd chicken out? Let the little girl make a fool out of herself, would you? Well now, Mr Grocery Clerk—she made a quick check of the baby. Some of the oatmeal had disappeared from her nose. Mr Grocery Clerk! Of course, a girl didn't have to be a genius to realise that was what he wasn't. Administrator? Executive? That seemed more likely. He was a man who recognised problems quickly and took care of them. The house, his cars, his manner of living, all of them spoke of money. Big money.

Yesterday, in the Harris living-room? Physical strength, yes. Determination, yes. Not the sort of man to be crossed. Thinking man? A grudging yes, and the water was splashing over the side of the tub like a flood!

'Hey, Mary, time to get out now!' Kitty came up to her knees and held out both hands.

'No!' The child sidled to the far side of the tub and shook her head sulkily. 'No, No, No! Baff!'

'That's all,' Kitty said, as sweetly as she knew how.

'No, no, no!' Mary replied, and started to cry. Kitty sat back on her heels again and sighed. There was no maintenance manual available for children. What to do next? Stand fast? Be firm? Stall? She fumbled for another towel and found she had used the last one on the wet floor. The nearest source of supply would then be in the hall cupboard. Stall!

'Watch the baby,' she ordered the dog. The big muzzle came up in almost a nod. Kitty checked them both for a minute. 'You be good,' she ordered the child. Mary responded at length.

Not exactly trusting either of them, Kitty raced down the hall to the right. The airing-cupboard door was stuck. It required some attention. When the door finally opened, Kitty grabbed a couple of towels blindly and raced back to the bathroom. The dog was gone. 'Mary?' The tub was empty. With heart in her mouth Kitty looked around wildly. It took her a moment to recognise the movement in the corner of the bathroom. The toilet-paper roll was spinning, and a trail led out of the bathroom door, down the hall to the stairs.

The National Football League could hardly have produced a runner as fast and agile as Katherine Anderson. She raced to the head of the stairs, and then grabbed at the newel post to steady herself. Halfway down the stairs Honey was keeping a careful eye on the baby. Mary, going down the stairs wet and naked in a backward crawl, clutched a handful of toilet paper in her little hand, and was singing wildly.

Mrs Wright was standing guard at the foot of the stairs, one of her big wooden spoons in her hands. For the first time in minutes Kitty took a deep breath. 'Good way to start the day!' Sara called. Kitty came slowly down the stairs, consulting her not-quite-waterproof wristwatch. Only sixty minutes of this day had gone by, and she was already exhausted.

Joel was back at exactly four o'clock, having driven at breakneck speed all the way down Highway Twenty-four. Mrs Wright met him at the door, instantly 'shushing' him. 'In the drawing-room,' she whispered. He eased past the cook, set his briefcase down, and peered into the room.

Squarely in the centre of the rug Mary was spread out, arms and legs thrown awry, fast asleep. Behind her, serving as a pillow, the giant mastiff opened one eye and then went back to sleep. Across the room from them

Kitty was sprawled out on the sofa, one foot still on the floor, her arm covered with some sort of pink lotion, also fast asleep.

'What in the——?' Joel started to say, when Sara Wright tugged at his sleeve and conducted him out of the room, closing the door behind her.

'You ought to be ashamed of yourself,' the cook said. 'The poor child!'

'Mary had a hard time?'

'Katherine had a hard time,' Mrs Wright replied. 'Worn to the bone, she is. Come to the kitchen.'

He followed her along, shedding coat and tie as he went, and begging a cup of coffee while she told the story. 'It was a quiet morning. The baby escaped from her bath and left a trail of wet and ruin all over the house. Kitty insisted on cleaning up. Then they went out to play. Next thing I knew, the pair of them were underneath your old car, changing the oil. Naturally Mary spilled the drainage can, and that required bath number two.'

'Neither of them looked too clean,' he protested. Sara gave him a glare.

'At lunchtime your darling niece was on her worst behaviour. I said peanut butter and jelly sandwiches, but Kitty had found a book—claimed it had to be a nutritious meal—and the first thing we knew the kitchen was in a mess, and that made bath number three. There was food all over the landscape, and Kitty insisted *she* had to clean it up. So while Mary napped, Kit worked.'

'And then?'

'And then somehow or another the mailman left the front door ajar, Mary escaped, and we all spent three hours hunting for her. Including Carswell.'

'Say, I've just noticed he's missing,' said Joel. 'Where the devil is he?'

'That's hard to say. During the hunt he fell and sprained his wrist. I sent him in to the emergency medical centre for treatment, and I haven't heard from him since.'

'I can't say he'll be missed. And then?' Joel leaned forward over the table, expecting the worst. And got it.

'And then Miss Kitty decided to put the dogs on the trail, and eventually they found Mary. She was playing hide-and-seek, sat down in the bushes down by the brook, and fell asleep again.'

'So that makes bath number four?' He chuckled, but the cook was not amused.

'Not until after——' She hesitated.

'After what?'

'The child was hiding in a patch of poison ivy. Mary isn't sensitive to it, but——'

'Oh, gawd,' he muttered. 'Kit and her allergies! Is that what's on her arm?'

'That's it,' Mrs Wright said bleakly.

'I think I'll have a whisky.' Shaking his head, he pushed away from the table and started for the library. Mail was piled high on the table. He fanned through it, found an envelope of interest, and was busy with its contents, tasting his second shot of whisky, when his brother walked in.

'Crazy afternoon.' John was pale, his hands trembling and his lower lip quivering. His brother toasted him as he looked up.

'I believe I'll have—just a touch of that,' John said defiantly, and made his way to the drinks cabinet. His nerves seemed to improve after the first swallow. 'That kid of yours——' he began.

'Of ours,' Joel interrupted.

'Yes—of ours. Got away this afternoon. Spent the afternoon looking for her. Tired.' He tossed off the remainder of his drink. 'And that girlfriend of yours isn't as recovered as you think she is. Worn to a frazzle, she was. Needs a hell of a lot more cherishing.' He got up and walked back over to the drinks cabinet. 'M'wife will kill me.' The second drink followed the first. 'I don't care.'

'Sit down,' ordered Joel. 'It's time we had a talk.'

John dropped his bulk into a chair. 'Don't know why,' he muttered.

'I think you do,' Joel replied. 'Be serious, man. You know I've had the auditors in.'

His brother got up and went back to the cabinet, bringing the bottle with him as he returned. 'So why tell me?'

'There's a shortage. Did you know about it?'

'Yes, I knew. How much?'

'Two hundred and fifty thousand dollars. A quarter of a million. Where did it go?'

'How the hell would I know? I didn't take it! I—how would *I* know how to fiddle the books?' muttered John.

'You'd be surprised to know I agree with you. You're too stupid to do something like this. But there's the disbursement notice. Look at the signature.'

The two brothers leaned towards each other as Joel dropped the paper on the adjoining small table. 'Not *my* signature,' John insisted. 'J Carmody? Not my signature. That's you, Joel.'

'Not my signature either,' Joel said softly. 'And now look at this.' He dropped another sheet of paper on top of the first. It was a handwritten letter, and boldly sprawled across the bottom was an identical 'J Carmody'.

His brother picked up the paper; his hands were trembling again. 'Where did you get this?' he muttered.

'Don't ask,' Joel returned. 'I've had a detective out looking. Read it, brother.'

'I—I don't want to.' John shuddered and almost dropped the note to the floor. 'I don't want to be mixed up in this, not for a minute I don't.'

'You're too late for that,' Joel said softly. 'You're in up to your neck. Read it.'

'It's addressed to Randolph. I——' Unable to avoid his brother's compelling gaze, John read on. '"There's a hundred thousand to be made from this housing project if we work it right. Fix those perk tests and get on with the permits. I don't intend my building project to collapse because you can't settle the problem in the DPW!" Signed, "J Carmody."'

John shuddered and gulped from the neck of the bottle. The note dropped to the table. Joel threw the rest of the envelope's contents down on top of it.

'Get a grip on yourself! There's no answer inside that bottle. You used to be a man, John. Be one again!' With that he got up angrily and walked out of the room, leaving his brother behind.

'A lot you know,' his younger brother said, but he recapped the bottle without pouring another drink.

'Dinner will be delayed for a few minutes,' Kitty apologised prettily. She was standing at the dining-room door. Inside the room Joel and Jessica were sharing drinks. 'Somehow or another I had to give Mary another bath, and——'

'That's four today?' Joel, with a teasing grin on his face, toasted her with his glass. Embarrassed, Kitty turned blush-red, then began to lose her temper.

'Five today,' she snapped. 'And it's all your fault!'

'Of course it is,' he responded, and took the wind out of her sails. 'I hear you had a hard time?'

'Did I ever!' she admitted, crossing the threshold. 'Mrs Wright is dressing the little—kid.'

'It sounds like an interesting day,' Jessica commented. 'Tell us about it.' Nothing loath, Kitty told them the whole story, complete with gestures. They both laughed all the way.

'I didn't think it was humorous at all at the time,' she concluded, then a broad grin broke out on her face. 'But now that I think it over, it is.' Joel walked over to the sideboard and poured her an orange juice. 'And I thought *anybody* could look after a kid!'

'That's what I've been telling Joel all this time,' Jessica declared. 'Taking care of children is a job for professionals.'

'Or mothers and fathers,' Joel interjected. 'I started adoption papers on Mary this morning. I'm going to adopt her.'

'And get control of her stock?' Jessica glared at him. 'Were none of us to be consulted?'

'I don't see why you should be,' he said slowly. 'Not after the fiasco with the corporation.' He sipped at his glass, then turned to Kit. 'Ever thought of being somebody's mother?'

'That requires somebody with a domestic sense. Which I haven't got,' Kitty admitted ruefully. 'What's that bit about the shoemaker sticking to his last? That's my way from now on.' She drained her glass, then added reflectively, 'Although I must say some parts of my day as a stand-in mother were a barrel of fun. She's a good child, Mary is.'

Which was Mrs Wright's cue to come to the door with the baby in her arms. A baby dressed in a neat pinafore, a bow in her silky red hair, and a big smile on her face. 'Dinner's ready,' the cook said. Joel moved forward to accept the child, and was saluted with a coquettish kiss.

'How is it possible?' Kitty murmured to Jessica as they started for the dining-room. 'This afternoon she was like a plague of locusts; now she looks as if butter wouldn't melt in her mouth!'

They gathered at the table without a sign of John. 'He wasn't feeling well,' Joel told Jessica. 'I gave him a couple of Panadols and he went off to bed. He has some problems.'

'Yes, I'm sure he has,' she replied.

And what do I make of all that? Kitty asked herself as she watched the interplay. Jessica looks so—subdued. As if she were trying to adjust to bad news. And the man next to her at table? He was watching his brother's wife like a hawk. And what do I make of *that*? she thought.

There wasn't time to find out. Mrs Wright brought in the roast beef and set it down in front of Joel. He promptly settled Mary in her special high-chair and fastened the straps while he tried to get the child to accept Kitty's attentions from the other side. The baby was willing, but there was no way she could get her little mouth around 'Aunt Kit'. She was willing to explain it all to 'Mama' with a very large incomprehensible statement as her uncle carved the meat. Mrs Wright collected the first slice and went back to the kitchen with it, returning moments later with a pile of carefully puréed roast beef to put on Mary's plate alongside the mashed potatoes.

'She can chew,' Sara reported defensively, 'but roast beef is hard for a child her age to handle. Are you listening, Kit?'

Kitty looked up from her own plate to find both Joel and Sara grinning at her. She shrugged her shoulders and filed it away under the title of 'Things that might be nice to know, but not very'. It was a pleasant meal, and the evening passed as enjoyably, but when Kitty wandered off to bed early, the thought was still puzzling her. Why would *I* want to know about the care and feeding of children? Unfortunately, she had little time available for that thought, because there were more important things to consider.

Am I any further ahead now than I was last night? she wondered. Who is the party I'm looking for? Joel had been such a likely prospect, but everybody agrees that he's only been here in Northport for a couple of weeks. The skulduggery has been going on for almost a year, maybe even longer. And then there was the spirited defence he had given her in the Harris home. No, probably Joel was safe. As Kitty thought that she was unable to suppress the smile. I *want* Joel to be on the good-guys list! she thought. The man is slowly getting under my skin!

So who does that leave? John, of course. Drunk or sober, John. Mrs Wright says John didn't always drink the way he does now. So he's in possession of a guilty conscience? Is that behind all his drinking? It was a question to be mulled over, to be thrashed out—but all it was doing at the present moment was keeping Kitty awake, and she needed her sleep. Somehow she had to take her mind off all her problems. A good book, that was the answer. And there was a whole library downstairs!

She shrugged herself into her robe and padded barefoot downstairs. The dogs lived outside in their own little houses; except for the wind rattling at a loose shutter the night was silent. The door to the library was half open. She stepped inside, closed the door behind her, and turned on the lights.

It was a strange sort of room, built like a slice of pie, to fit in between the double chimneys of the old construction, and the dining-room. Several overstuffed chairs were scattered over the thick rug. All the walls were covered with bookcases from floor to ceiling. All the cases were full. Leather bindings with gold inscriptions glared at her from all directions. The single window, at the pointed end of the pie-slice facing out over the hill, was uncurtained. A storm-moon sent a ray or two through the thick bottle-glass.

'But all I want is a paperback thriller,' Kitty mourned. The library glared at her as if its dignity had been assailed. She wandered around the perimeter, searching. The only possibility seemed to be a pile of papers on the end table near the window. It was either that or *The History of Zamboanga*, which, a quick exploration told her, was published in 1896.

'Not a good year for books,' she told herself as she settled into the chair next to the end-table and began to thumb through the papers.

It was the envelope that captured her attention. 'Whaling City Investigations', she saw. Joel's detective agency. More surveillance reports? Kitty had been raised in a strict Lutheran society, so she knew better. One did not read other people's mail! But nothing less than the appearance of a burning bush was going to keep her from perusing *this* mail. Eager hands fumbled; the envelope itself skidded out of her hands and landed on the floor. And there, uncovered, was a facsimile of a handwritten note. She picked it up. 'Dear Randolph,' it began. Her unbelieving eyes traced all the words, and came to a halt on the signature. 'J Carmody.'

The world closed in on Kitty. Sight and sound were shut out. For a moment her head rocked dizzily. A pain developed in her stomach, and spread throughout her system. And then anger, slowly rising anger, began to grow. As it spread it suppressed everything else. Her mind cleared. She could not remember a time when she saw things so clearly, so precisely. Here in her hand was the 'smoking gun'. Here was the positive proof she had been searching for all this time. And the man responsible! He hadn't needed to be here on the ground. Conspiracies could be accomplished by mail as well!

For a moment she doubted. Why would a man as obviously intelligent as Joel put his signature on a document like this? Why would a man she loved so much do this to her? But theory clashed with fact. There it was, a bold scrawl across the paper. She could feel a gradual chill spread outward from her stomach into all her veins. A terrible cloak of loneliness fell upon her. For such a short time she had known friendship, love, excitement. And now, only bitter tears and loneliness. Her anger claimed her.

She stomped back up the stairs to her room and slammed the door behind her. No one noticed. There was nothing she wanted more than to have that—that man come into her room so she could tell him what she thought of him! But if he did, could she avoid the hypnotic voice, the charisma? Of course he would lie! And the only thing for *me* to do, she told herself grimly, is to go home. Right now. No waiting for confrontations, no more words. The syllogism sprang to mind: all men tell lies. Joel is a man. Therefore, Joel tells lies. She knew the fallacy inherent there, but meant to deny it.

It took her barely ten minutes to dress, and another ten to throw what she could into the single bag in her wardrobe. It meant taking less than half of her clothes with her, but walking in the dark made a light load imperative. One last check of the room. The note itself— the evidence—that she *had* to take with her. With considerably more care than she had used on her clothes she folded the paper and put it securely in her breast pocket. One more look around; she dashed away the tear that was forming. The bag was heavier than she had expected. She hefted it with both hands and went silently out into the corridor and closed the door behind her.

All the other doors were closed—with one exception. Down in the far corner, opposite Joel's room, the nursery door was half open. Kitty set her bag down by the head of the stairs and walked silently down the hall.

A night-light cast shadows in the baby's room. Mary no longer occupied a crib. Her low youth-bed had a rail all the way around, but only high enough to keep her from rolling off on to the floor. The child was asleep on her stomach, as usual, clutching a teddy bear almost as big as she was. Her mouth was open, and she bubbled as she breathed. Something caught at Kitty's heart.

She glided over to the bedside. Her hand—the one without the poison ivy rash—came up without orders and stroked the glistening hair. The baby grumbled but did not stir. I don't know what's gotten into me, Kitty told herself. Why would I have this crazy feeling about the niece of a monster? And not even a cute baby, at that!

But it was there. Deep in one corner of her heart—a corner previously unused—was this tenuous feeling. She stuck her index finger down into the child's balled fist, and felt the automatic tightening as Mary returned the pressure. For another moment Kitty left her finger there, then reluctantly withdrew it. Mary whimpered. Kitty held her breath, but the baby did not stir.

One more moment. The big clock downstairs struck twice. The wind rattled at the loose shutter again. Kitty brushed another tear away as she bent low over the bed and kissed the soft smooth forehead. 'Goodbye, kid,' she whispered over the lump that was blocking her throat, and forced herself to hurry out of the room.

Across the hall was the closed door of Joel's room. Her hand went to the knob and then was snatched back. *He* won't feel the way I do, she told herself. He has plenty of friends, and a family to fall back on, and he probably won't even notice I'm gone. Lord, how have I mixed myself up with that crazy kid and her lying nuncle? The question was impossible to answer. Tears blinded her as she made for the stairs.

The wind tried to snatch the front door out of her hands as she opened it. She dropped her bag and managed to two-hand it shut behind her. Clouds were obscuring some of the stars and all of the crescent moon. There was hardly enough light to see by, but she resolutely fumbled around for the handles of the bag.

It was not a handle she found. It was a cold nose, a rough tongue and a swishing sound that indicated a tail wagging. Honey. Kitty pushed his nose aside, found her bag, and took a couple of steps off on to the gravel. The dog followed. 'Stay!' she hissed, pointing back to the Carmody house. The huge mastiff licked at her finger and followed at a respectable distance.

'Go home,' said Kitty as she stopped in the open fields some hundred yards from the house. The dog sat down, eyes glued on her, and gave a sharp bark. Kitty went back and hushed him, kneeling down to place herself on eye level.

'Look, you crazy dog,' she explained, 'you've got a good home, plenty to eat—the best of everything. Why follow me around? I'm a loser!' The dog woofed again. 'And don't do that! I don't want everyone in the house following me!' Honey whimpered, and pawed at her with one huge forepaw. Kitty stood up and brushed off her skirt.

'I don't care *what* you think,' she told him crossly. 'I don't like dogs! Go home!' But when she turned her back on him and resolutely continued her walk down the hill the dog followed right along. At a respectful distance, of course.

She was awakened just after sunrise. The room, the whole house, seemed foreign to her. Bleary-eyed, she followed the source of the noise. Just outside the door Honey was sitting, squirming, and whimpering.

'Well, I told you to go home,' Kitty grumbled. 'Dumb dog!' But she made a tactical mistake. She held the screen door half open while she discussed philosophy, and before the last words were out the huge mastiff had slipped by her and was in the kitchen, a very wise look on his face.

'Look, if you think I've become a patsy for some dog half the size of a horse, you've got another think coming,' she lectured. The dog squirmed closer to her. Reluctantly her hand went down and caressed the rough-coated head. Honey barked and sat back. Even a *dumb* dog knew when he had won!

Being up, Kitty decided to make a day out of it. She went into the bathroom and managed a lukewarm shower, then grumbled as she searched around the hot-water heater. Some kindly soul had turned her thermostat almost to the off position. Breakfast was a haphazard thing. Usually she ate left-overs for breakfast. That same someone who had turned down her thermostat had also cleaned out her refrigerator, and the propane refrigerator unit had to have its pilot light relit. The only thing left in her larder was cornflakes. She spooned out a bowlful, but found that eating cornflakes without milk was difficult. Even the dog refused it.

'You see how stupid I am?' she addressed the animal. 'Any sensible person would have waited until after breakfast to run off. But not me! I don't have the smarts for that! Which is one *more* reason for you to get out of here. Get! Scoot! Go home!' She laid a trail to the front door. Honey followed along at her heels. But when she held the door open for the animal and yelled at it a couple more times, the beast, instead of stepping by her and walking away, butted into her buttocks with his heavy head and pushed *her* out on to the steps. And then had the colossal nerve to sit inside in the shade and bark at her through the closed screen door.

'Now wait just a darn minute!' she yelled.

'Just what *I* wanted to say,' the voice behind her said. She whirled around. Joel stood there, resting a hip against the apple tree, staring at her. Her first thought was, Here I am outside in the sun and wearing only my nightgown! And her second thought was, And with the sun shining on it, this gown is about as transparent as a plate of glass! She stabbed one hand at the doorknob, to find his there before her.

'Oh, no, you don't,' he said. 'You don't slip out on me.'

'Leave me alone,' she muttered, backing away from him. Honey barked at them both.

'So that's where you've gotten,' he commented to the dog. 'Well, lady, that's a thoroughbred dog, valued at over five hundred dollars. Stealing items of that value in the Commonwealth is a felony. Dognapping. For all I know there may be a mandatory life sentence.'

'Don't be a wise guy,' she railed at him. 'I'm in no mood for your terrible puns. I didn't kidnap your dog—he followed me all the way. I think probably you abuse him, or something. Get off my property!'

'Not until you tell me why, Kit.' Joel had her hands imprisoned in his by that time, pulling her closer, to the point where their bodies almost touched.

'Why what?' She ducked her head. Angry as she was, there was something about this man that she was unwilling to face.

'You're not well enough to live by yourself, Kit. Why did you run away in the middle of the night?'

'Because I was struck with an attack of common sense!' she snapped at him. 'Let me go, you—you! Turn me loose!'

'Not until you tell me why,' he insisted. She had to summon up more anger to overcome the sweetness of his tone.

'Tell you why? You know why. I'll show you why.' Using all her strength, she managed to break one hand free and open the door. His dog growled at him as they went by, Kitty in the lead, towing. In the kitchen she turned around again and glared at him. Reluctantly he released her other wrist. The facsimile note was on her kitchen table. She snatched it and thrust it in his face. 'That's why!' she shouted at him.

Joel backed away from the flame of her anger, a perplexed look on his face. 'Where did you get that?'

'In your library!' she yelled. 'I went down to get a book to read, and found a whole damn conspiracy. Joel Carmody. J Carmody. It could hardly be written any bigger. I know who you are now, Mr Carmody. And as soon as I can contact my lawyer I'm going to get even with you!'

'Katherine.' His voice was low, but there was a tiny quaver in it. She noted the fierce gleam in his eye, and became silent. They formed a little tableau, the three of them, Kitty and Joel each trying to watch the other, the dog trying to watch them both.

'Do you really believe I signed that paper, Katherine?'

Her face froze into a stubborn grimace. 'I do!' A little thought at the back of her mind whispered, Don't believe it, Kit. He's a good man. She caught her breath, then suppressed the wild reminder. Fact. He *had* signed the paper.

She cleared her throat. 'Yes, I do.' Firmly said. The dog whimpered. Deny it, Kitty screamed at him silently. Deny it, Joel! Explain how it needn't be! Tell me it's all a mistake and you love me.

Instead he shoved both his hands in his pockets, gave her a speculative look, and turned on his heel. 'Then there doesn't seem to be anything else to say,' he commented. 'Come on, Honey.' The mastiff grumbled deep in his throat, but followed his master out of the door.

The screen door slammed behind them like the punctuation on a life sentence.

'Oh lord,' Kitty moaned, 'what have I done?' She fell back into one of the kitchen chairs and the tears fell.

CHAPTER EIGHT

THERE was a succession of gloomy days, both in the skies and in Kitty's heart. Over and over she wrestled with the facts. Over and over her mental jury brought in the guilty verdict. Over and over her heart cried, mourning over those few sweet days she had shared with Joel. Loneliness followed her everywhere she went, like a tiny dark cloud that rained only on her. So she dragged around the old farmhouse each morning, cleaning, re-arranging the furniture. Most afternoons she spent out in the barn, overhauling her farm machinery. One after-noon she thought she heard a child's voice in the dis-tance, up by the brook, and came racing out of the barn to see. It was a false alarm. But as regular as clockwork every morning, promptly at sunrise, Honey appeared at her front door and took up guard duty.

'You're a fool, you know,' she told the animal on the fourth day as she wheeled out her ten-speed bicycle. Ordinarily she would have fed the dog some left-overs, but the cupboard was bare this time. 'Go home. Please?' The dog raised his head from the cool slate of the doorstep and barked once at her. Kitty shrugged her shoulders.

She checked to be sure that the basket on the back of her bike was fastened securely, and readjusted the straps on her backpack. That's one of the million little things he was right about, she told herself. Groceries *are* heavy. And it was a two-mile ride from the Neck to the super-market. She slid her foot into the pedal clip and started down the drive. The dog got up and ambled along behind her.

'No!' she ordered as she came to a stop at the road entrance. The dog stopped too, sitting down in the dust of the driveway, panting. 'Go home!' she shouted at him. He gave her a little yip. When she started off again he came along as well.

There was a young man standing at the junction of her drive and the main road—some six feet or more, thin, earnest, sandy-haired. He held up his hand and called to her. Kitty squeezed the brakes and put one foot down. She knew the boy, but could not remember where she had met him. Honey was up beside her before she could come to a stop; in front of her, in fact, with his lips drawn back from those massive teeth and a growl rumbling deep in his throat.

'Down!' Kitty commanded. The dog came to a watching halt. The young man took a deep breath.

'Miss Anderson, I'm Ed Harris, from across the street. You remember me?'

How could I not? she asked herself. This is the young man Joel picked up with one hand and bounced off the wall! 'Yes, I remember.' A cool statement of fact, with no emotions involved. He took a half-step forward, but stopped when Honey growled again.

'I wanted to tell you how sorry I am that we caused you so much trouble,' he said.

'We?' she queried.

'We. Me and a bunch of the neighbourhood kids. They're too young to realise how serious a problem it all is. They just came along for the fun of it.'

Unsure, but impressed by his serious approach, Kit paused. 'Did your father send you over here to apologise?'

'My father doesn't have a thing to do with it,' the boy insisted. 'Well, maybe I said that wrong. I suppose it was hearing my father discuss things with my mother that prompted everything. Do you realise, Miss Anderson, how frightened the people in this subdivision are about you and your legal stuff? They all have a substantial part of their incomes tied up in these houses, and you're threatening to have the whole place torn down!'

'Me?' she queried. 'Where did you hear that?'

'Oh, I don't know. I heard it in a couple of places down in the village. And then it spread around like a ground fire. Rumours do that, you know.'

'I don't know anything about tearing down houses,' Kitty mused, 'so how could anyone else?'

'Francis sounded pretty sure,' the boy maintained. 'And his father's right up there in the Government.'

'Francis who?'

'Why, Francis Randolph, of course.'

Francis Randolph. The name clicked into place in Kitty's mental jigsaw puzzle. The son of the first selectman. The man Joel had hired a detective agency to follow around. It doesn't take me long to realise that two and two make four, she told herself—provided I'm hit over the head enough times.

'I don't know what's going to happen,' she told the youth. 'But I *do* know that I've no plans to have anything torn down. You can tell your father that, if you want to. And I thank you for coming over to talk to me.' She extended her hand. For a moment Ed Harris hesitated, then he seized it and, with a big grin on his face, shook it vigorously. It was only then that Kitty realised there were a dozen or more people, from children to ancients, watching them from across the street.

'C'mon, Honey,' she commanded gruffly, and started to pedal down the road. The mastiff sniffed around Ed Harris for a second, then dashed down the road after her. She pushed along at a leisurely pace. Her original intention had been to speed down the road to lose the dog. Now she felt better knowing those big teeth and massive jaws were on her side, and only a few feet behind.

They wheeled along the gradual slope that led down to the Hopkins Neck bridge. The wind picked at her and teased; the clouds covered the sun and cooled the air. A flock of seagulls hovered over the docks across the river, where the fishing-boats were unloading. It was an altogether nice day, and she might have been exuberant, but somehow Joel Carmody's face kept haunting her. Joel, and that lovable little kid. Joel, and those warm arms. Joel, who didn't seem to mind being in love with the town grouch!

She pulled off to the side of the road for a moment. A pair of perfectly formed teardrops were blinding her. As she cleared her eye with her knuckle a fisherman standing on the bridge with his line in the water waved to her. She responded as she went by.

Not until she had manoeuvred up the hill and turned right on to Main Street did it strike her. There weren't a large number of fish available off the bridge. People who knew the neighbourhood went over to the other side of the river. So why in the world was Lieutenant Frankel of the State police standing out there in dungarees, a T-shirt and an old straw hat, fishing where no fish ran?

The question troubled her until she came up in front of the Safehaven market, and parked her bike. Safehaven wasn't the biggest market in the world, and perhaps supermarket was too strong a word for it, but either you shopped at Safehaven or you drove ten miles to the Malls in Dartmouth. With no car, Kitty's options were limited. She set the bike up on its kickstand outside the big double doors.

'Guard,' she ordered. Honey wagged his tail and sat down about three feet away from the vehicle. Not knowing what else to say to a mastiff, Kitty patted him on the head and went into the store.

There was a small crowd of shoppers at work—perhaps twenty or so. Kitty was too busy with her own worries to pay any attention to them. She snatched at a shopping cart and began her tour. Staples were what she needed. Cans and boxes. Soup and spaghetti and soap and toilet paper and bread. And four quarts of skimmed milk. Nothing from the delicatessen; none of the specialities. Just staples. She wheeled up and down the aisles, her head turning right and left automatically, not paying any attention to the other shoppers. So when the baby screamed 'Mama!' right in her ear she jumped, and dropped the can of fruit juice she was considering. Mary Carmody was riding in the back of the adjacent shopping cart, and Sara Wright was at the wheel.

The word startled Kitty, and amused half a dozen other people in the same aisle. The baby struggled to her feet, stretched out both hands, and wiggled her fingers in a 'come-here' summons. When Kitty failed to move, almost frozen in place, the child took an additional step straight ahead, right off the edge of her cart. Which was enough to impel Kitty forward in time to catch her.

Held securely and safely against Kitty's shoulder, Mary babbled at double speed, with an occasional word coming clear—like Nuncle Joe, or birdie, or Mama. It was a very involved presentation. 'She misses you,' Sara contributed.

'Well!' Kitty cleared her throat and handed the baby back. 'I'm sure she'll get over it.' And why is it so hard to maintain my cool? she asked herself. So Mary is a nice kid. The world is full of them. And I suspect her uncle put her up to this 'Mama' business. 'How come you're stuck with the baby, Sara?' she asked.

'Stuck? Bite your tongue, Katherine. I *enjoy* having her with me. It's a stroke of good luck!'

'Yeah, sure,' Kitty muttered. And then, more vigorously, 'I thought her uncle never wanted hired hands to look after her?'

'An exception.' Sara grinned and winked. 'He had something that only *he* can do. Keeps him out all hours of the night, it does. Comes home at breakfast time, eats, gets a nap—and off he goes again.'

'I didn't know the grocery business required those hours. He's going to ruin his health!' Even Kitty's ears heard the wistful ending to the sentence. Sara grinned at her again.

'That's my girl!' she laughed. 'The words say I don't care, but the music sings a different tune!'

'Nonsense,' Kitty averred. 'Pure nonsense!'

'We'll see, my dear. Himself says it'll all be over in a couple of days, and you'll be back with us.'

'He's got rocks in his head.' Kitty fumbled for words to cover her surprise. I'll be back with them? What a laugh *that* is. I wonder how that man keeps a single grocery store open, never mind a bunch of them! Or was it because he was working on some bigger conspiracy, some larger confidence game? She glanced up. Sara was about to tell her something more that she didn't want to hear.

'I've got to go,' Kitty announced gruffly, and turned her cart towards the cash registers. Behind her she could hear the child's litany. 'G'bye, Mama! G'bye! G'bye!' The words haunted her; she didn't even count the change, but hurried out into the afternoon with a monkey on her back.

A group of young men were gathered in a half-circle around her bicycle, which had fallen over on its side. Young, in comparison to Kitty's own stately age. The five of them might run from eighteen to twenty, with one obvious leader who might well be over twenty-five.

'Hey, babe.' He stepped forward out of the crowd, a head taller than the others, brown hair, athletic build showing under a T-shirt and shorts. He appeared to be the sort who would pump iron for a hobby.

'Yes?' It was her best put-down style. After all, what could he hope to accomplish in the middle of Main Street? Kitty subdued her nervousness in her own fashion. Chocolate cookie, she told herself. Which was a code word for a person who was all marshmallow on the inside, but with a hard, almost impenetrable skin.

'You remember me? Francis.'

'Can't say I do, sonny. Was there something you wanted? Francis what?'

'Francis Randolph.' He was somewhat taken aback by her response, but mustered up a little more bravado. 'I've been out to your house a couple of times.'

'Have you really? I trust you enjoyed the trip?'

'Don't smart-mouth me, lady. I know all about you.'

'Good, then we needn't continue this stupid conversation any further.'

'Yeah, I remember. Actions speak louder than words—that's your gig, isn't it? Well, how about a little action?'

He raised his foot and smashed it down on her front wheel. With the bike already resting on its side, and the spokes of the wheel carefully tightened, he did no damage at all—except to his pride. But having taken the first step, he felt bound by his peculiar sense of honour to do something more. And his group was urging him on. He looked around at them all with a big grin on his face, and stooped to pick the bicycle up. It was, though he couldn't know it at the time, the end of the line.

Honey had moved over to the other side of the boardwalk, up against the wall itself, where he could find some shade from the now brilliant sun. When Francis Randolph bent over the big mastiff rose, stretched, and walked with stiff legs over to where the action was.

The youth had Kitty's bicycle in both hands, about to raise it over his head, when Honey slumped down beside him. The dog's jaws closed around his ankle, just hard enough for him to realise there was something there. The bike came down on its wheels. Kitty grabbed the handlebars and wheeled it out of the way. The youth's mouth was half open as he looked down at the size and shape of the dog, and felt the prickly penetration of those teeth.

'Hey!'

'Don't yell,' Kitty advised him. 'Honey is getting old, and tends to be nervous about loud noises.' All lies, of course. Even Honey gave her an insulted look before he turned back to the object in hand—one ankle bone.

'You—he's your dog?'

'I thought you knew everything about me? No, he's not *my* dog exactly.'

'Call him off!' wailed Francis.

'Don't get desperate, sonny. He's not really doing any harm. And since he's not my dog, I don't quite know how to call him off! For all I know he hasn't eaten in a week. Dogs are great ones for gnawing on bones, aren't they.'

'I——' Nothing had happened. No loud noises, no deep bites, no growls, but Francis Randolph was frightened half to death. His face was white, and perspiration was running down both cheeks. His erstwhile friends had all backed away, hoping the animal wouldn't select another target.

'Maybe you ought to just go home,' Kitty suggested.

'But he——'

'He might let go if you asked him properly.'

'I—— Dog? Let go, dog?'

'The magic word,' Kitty suggested.

'P-Please?'

Kitty, who didn't know the command that would get the dog to release him, compromised by kneeling down and scratching Honey behind his left ear. It seemed to do the trick. The dog's mouth opened slightly, and the youth was off and down the street. Sara Wright came out of the store at just that moment, intending to take her cart over to her car. She saw the commotion, and came over to where Kitty was standing.

'What's the trouble?' she asked.

'I'm not sure I know,' Kitty answered as she forced a blatantly fake perplexed look on to her face. 'There was something about my bicycle that annoyed him.'

'If you say so,' Sara reflected, and nodded her head. 'So that's where Honey's been getting to. He's been missing every day. Don't tell me you're going to take all those groceries home on a bicycle?'

'It was my original intention,' said Kitty, sighing. 'But I could be talked out of it!'

'It really is nice, having rich friends with cars,' Kitty announced to her house some hours later. She was lying in the bathtub, having filled it to the brim with warm water. The heat relaxed all her tense muscles as she slid herself down deep into the suds.

Sara had driven her home, stayed for a few minutes for coffee and conversation, and had gone on home, taking the baby and the dog with her. It should be said that neither apparently wanted to go.

All the groceries were stacked in the cupboards. Unfortunately those cupboards had been built by her grandfather to hold food for a large family, so her tiny purchases of the day, although enough for her needs, huddled in corners and looked very lonely. But she had made an interesting supper for herself, washed the dishes, walked the perimeter of her possessions, and thence went directly to the bath. It was good to relax.

If only I could shut off my brain, she thought. I wonder what brother Robert's doing now? How far away is Africa? Does he think and plan and wonder about home? Somewhere in the back of her mind there was a nagging doubt. She wrote to her brother irregularly; he had answered only three times in the year he had been away. What if—what if, after all the strains and troubles she had gone through to knit his heritage back together, he really didn't *want* to come back?

She shrugged herself upright, watching the suds slowly drain down off her breasts and disappear among the million bubbles at her side. Robert. A kind, sensitive older brother, with none of the brashness of the rest of the Andersons. And none of the spirit and strength either. An older brother who, in their schooldays, had been more than willing to have his tough-minded little sister do his fighting for him!

Suppose he decides, out there in far-off Africa, never to come back to New England? she thought. Never to take up the land that Grandfather Anderson had sweated and strained to in-gather. Suppose all that? Then everything I've done would be wasted! Totally wasted. The thought was a shock. She scrambled to her feet, pulled the drain plug, and turned on the shower to rinse herself.

It was a restless, fatigued woman who dried herself off in the worn bath-towel, spent twenty minutes with towel and brush on her lovely long blonde hair, then pulled her long white nightgown over her head.

Sleep was obviously impossible. She made herself a cup of hot cocoa and took it along to the bedroom. Books there were galore, all well read. She was in no mood for a thrice-told tale. She stretched out on the bed, her back against three pillows, and sipped the warm drink. Through her mind ran a series of pictures. Robert, fair-haired like any Swede, laughing at her as he waved goodbye. Joel, bright and smiling, with a halo of sunlight around his head, beckoning to her. Sara, a wooden stirring spoon in her hand, shaking her head in a vaguely disgusted way. Baby Mary, suddenly transferred into a Rhodes Scholar, with cap and gown and a vocabulary bigger than Webster. Honey, alternately growling and whining at her, running a few steps up the hill and then returning when she failed to follow him on the path that led home. Home?

It was all too much. She swung her feet down on to the floor and sorted through the half-dozen medicine bottles on her bedside table. One of them was a mild sleeping pill. 'For pain,' Becky Meadows had said severely. But wasn't all this pain? Perhaps not physical, but pain nevertheless. Kitty shrugged her shoulders and took three of the tiny tablets before she stretched out again on the bed. A wild dream pursued her. Katherine Anderson standing outside the VFW Hall on a snowy night, pressing her nose against the windowpane, watching the entire town inside, dancing in the warmth and conviviality, while Kitty shivered, all alone, outside.

Joel Carmody came home to the house on the hill at about eleven o'clock. He was tired. It had been a long day, and the night before had been longer, but he finally held the solution in his hands. Strange, he thought as he muddled his way through the cold supper Mrs Wright had left. Two major problems, and the one solution fitted them both. Not a pleasant solution, but then——

Irritated at his own thoughts, he refilled his coffee mug and took it with him into the library, where the one window in the room looked out over the hill, over the farmhouse down there in the gloom. He pulled a heavy chair up and sat down, as he had done for many a night since Kitty had walked out of his life.

There was a gleam in one of the windows down there. The kitchen, he thought, or maybe the bathroom. As he watched it went out, to reappear at the back of the house in what he knew was her bedroom. It glowed there for almost an hour.

At twelve o'clock he pulled up the little portable radio he wore clipped to his belt, a loan from the State police barracks. Eventually Lieutenant Frankel announced himself at the other end of the electronic circuit. 'Some trouble down here,' the metallic-sounding voice said. 'A big triple accident on I-195. I had to pull the man off the bridge-watch.'

'Everything looks peaceful here,' Joel reported. 'And I got those two papers we were talking about. Maybe tomorrow we could have a pow-wow?'

'That's a Roger,' the police detective assured him. 'After I get some sleep.' Joel, still watching, noticed that the light had gone out in the bedroom down below him. He signed out of the police net, walked to the front door and whistled softly. In a moment Honey was nuzzling at his hand. He patted the dog's head, walked with him to the corner of the house, and pointed down the hill. 'Go,' he commanded. 'Guard!' The dog took a few tentative steps downhill and turned to face him, questioningly.

If Kitty knew the dog had been *sent* rather than just *came*, she would have screamed blue murder, he thought. It brought a grin to his face. 'Go!' he repeated. The big dog whined, then got up, turning slowly back down the hill. A few steps further on he stopped again, facing downhill, one front paw off the ground. The mastiff sniffed the air, whined again, then burst out into a fury of barking. A moment later the animal went crashing down the hill in full spate, baying as he went.

It took a moment or two before Joel could gather his wits. His eyes had told him a truth he didn't want to believe. A flare of flame had coasted through the air down there below him and landed on the front porch of the farmhouse. A motor roared as some sort of truck made a U-turn in Kitty's driveway and went roaring up the road. And in another moment flame was licking at the front of the old wooden house.

Frantically he snatched at the radio at his belt. Lieutenant Frankel was still available. 'Somebody's just torched the house!' he yelled into the transceiver. 'A truck. Maybe more than one, heading for the bridge. Call the fire department!' He didn't wait for an answer, but re-hung the radio at his belt and went plunging down the hill in Honey's wake. Before he reached the brook he could hear the fire siren from the village as it summoned the volunteer firemen.

Honey was already at the house, circling around, baying. As Joel came through the trees he started to yell Kitty's name, but there was no response. By the time he reached the barn the front of the house was aflame. The old wood, some of it in place since 1718, offered no resistance. There was only a small breeze, which offered some help, but not much.

Remembering the light in her bedroom, Joel went up to the back windows. They were open, but heavily screened. He tried vainly to peer in, but to no avail. The thick screens made it impossible for him to claw his way inside. A quick run around the house showed he could not enter from either the front or the side doors. Desperate, his mind filled with pictures he did not want to admit, he turned around and ran for the barn. The big aluminium door was padlocked, and he had not thought to bring his picks with him. A large rock lying beside the building provided the answer. With the adrenalin he had running he might have been able to smash a hole in the side of the building; the padlock was an easy victim.

He was back at the house within a minute. Smoke was eddying out of the bedroom window in front of him. He raised the axe.

'Not that one!' a voice at his elbow yelled. 'Volunteer fireman. Get the *other* window. Divert the smoke away from the bed!' It sounded like good advice. Joel moved down to the corner window and began chopping. Three minutes seemed like a long time in the face of an emergency. It took that length of time for him to batter his way into the bedroom. The room was full of smoke, hanging at a level just an inch or two above her bed. And Kitty lay there, fast asleep, but twisting and turning and wheezing as the smoke teased at her asthma. On the nearby bureau he spotted a pair of her medical inhalators and jammed them into his pocket.

'Kit!' he shouted. No response. He jumped to the window and passed the axe out. The volunteer fireman, holding a heavy spotlight, pointed it into the room. The smoke was barrelling out of the window behind him, the one he had smashed. Back beside the bed he snatched Kitty up in his arms; there was no time for thought, for fear. He brushed the hair out of her face and rushed her to the second window, where screen and window-frame had fallen under the axe. More hands were available outside. They cradled Kitty gently, and two figures hurried her away from the building.

'Hurry up!' the man outside yelled at him. 'The roof is—— '

The warning was a second too late. The roof fell in, collapsing on to the bed in a fiery sheet of flame. The bedcovers ignited immediately, hanging a wall of flame between him and the only available window. He took a quick look around, then committed himself. The blocking flames were only a foot or two from the wall.

He lined himself up on the faint gleam of the spotlight outside, then hurled himself forward, going through the flame and the window while in the air, and somersaulting on to the ground. Water splashed at him as a couple of men doused him with buckets of the stuff. Then they grabbed him under the arms and hurried him away towards the barn, where they set him down beside Kitty's recumbent form.

He took a deep ragged breath and turned towards the woman who meant so much to him. She was still asleep, her lungs clearing in the fresh night air, but the bubbling in her throat was more noticeable.

Joel dropped to the ground and caught her up in his arms, forcing the feed unit of one of the inhalators between her teeth. 'Breathe!' he commanded hoarsely. And she did.

Asthma was a strange disease. Under proper treatment the effects seemed to evaporate—as they did here. She lay back against him with a silly little smile on her face, purring as if the dream that enveloped her was very pleasant indeed.

'I don't make that out at all,' he said to one of the firemen, soot-covered, who came over to squat down beside him. 'But luckily some of you fire people were close by.'

'No trouble at all,' Mr Harris said as he pulled off his fireman's hat and wiped his brow. 'We only live across the street, and my son keeps late hours.' He waved his hand vaguely in the direction of the house, where his son Edward, similarly clothed, was making a careful examination.

Joel shook his head. 'Kit will never believe this,' he muttered.

'Oh, I think she will,' said Harris. By this time his son had come over to them.

'Nothing much we can do until the pumper gets here,' the boy reported. 'There's no water laid on, and everything is tinder-dry. I'm afraid the whole house is going to go!'

'It's not important,' Joel told them. 'Just so long as we've got *her* out of there. Arson, I suppose?'

'Arson. No doubt about it.'

'I'm gonna kill somebody!' His tongue felt the bitterness. He pounded one big fist into the other, and his rage grew to enormous proportions. Until he saw her figure, faint-white in the light of the fire, move. Everything fell away from him but love. With cautious hands he cradled her on his lap. She sighed and nestled close against his shoulder without opening her eyes. 'Joel,' she murmured, as if his name meant everything in the world to her. A rough tongue licked at his hands; Honey had come to join the celebration.

As had the volunteer fire department. Eighteen minutes from the first alarm, with the equipment almost three miles from the fire, the ancient pumper came up the driveway, its sirens screaming, its red and yellow lights flashing. It took but two minutes more to set up, and water began pouring out of the pumper's tank. Kitty nestled on Joel's shoulder through it all.

About half an hour after their arrival the fire department's chief came around the ruin and joined them on the hillside. 'Not much we can do,' he reported. The EMTs from the ambulance that followed quickly on the heels of the pumper were working on Joel's arms. Kitty was still asleep.

'You've done well to save the outbuildings,' said Joel. 'Nobody could fault your responses, and I intend to tell the town just that. Ouch!'

'Sorry,' the young medical technician apologised. 'Can't see too well here. These burns aren't too serious, sir.' That was one thing that Joel hated. Having grown past thirty, to have a bright young man call him 'sir' grated on his nerves. But he did his best to pass it off.

'And Kit?' he asked, holding his breath before the answer.

'In good shape,' the young technician reported. 'No burns. The smoke has cleared from her lungs. Asthmatic, is she? All her vital signs are excellent. If I were to guess, I'd say the lady took more than one sleeping pill before she went to bed!'

'Well, I'll be double-damned, dyed blue, and tossed into sheep dip!' Joel exclaimed. All three men, looking at each other across the body of the sleeping woman, grinned at each other.

One of the water-drenched firemen came up to join him, with a pair of containers in his hands. 'Gasoline, chief,' he reported. 'It's all over the porch. You can smell it everywhere.'

'Be careful of the handles,' the chief ordered. 'Fingerprints aren't impossible. Tag them both and put them in the trunk of my car.'

'And now, Mr Carmody, perhaps you could tell me who hates the little lady enough to set fire to her house?'

Joel was about to say something when the radio transceiver at his belt rattled and beeped at him. He pulled the instrument up to where he and the chief both could hear.

'Lieutenant Frankel,' the distorted voice on the radio identified itself. 'We got them at the bridge. Triumph of stupidity—four men in a truck, trying to get over the only bridge on the only road out of the area. Two full cans of gasoline in the back seat. What about your end?'

'This is Chief Osman,' the fire chief said. 'The house is a dead loss. All the other buildings are safe. Gasoline here too—two empty cans. I'll be bringing them along for you to fingerprint. Definitely a case of arson. Don't let some smart lawyer get those four out of your hands until I can talk to them.'

'I can do that,' Frankel advised. 'How's the girl?'

Joel took over the microphone. 'She's better than you and I are,' he reported. 'She's still fast asleep. I think she'll weather the storm OK.'

'Fast asleep? Well, I'll be——'

'I might be too,' said Joel, laughing. 'This whole affair is getting curiouser and curiouser. Do you suppose we could have a conference at my house tomorrow? Maybe our lady will be awake by mid-afternoon.'

'That'll be nice,' the police lieutenant replied, and signed off.

'Not much more I can do here,' Chief Osman reported. 'I'll leave one company and the pumper until they're sure the ashes have cooled down. And I think I'll go have a talk with the district attorney.'

'So why not?' Joel returned. 'I think I'll just sit here and enjoy myself.'

'All night?'

'Well, as I'm sure the little lady would say if she were conscious, why not?'

There was some confusion as the firemen left. A few had come on the pumper; most of the others had driven to the site in their own cars. But gradually they filtered off, until the six men of Engine Company Four were all that were left. The fire had died away to a crackle. There was nothing left of the house but the pile of embers, and a few heavy timbers from the roof. The heat-storm had passed away, although there was considerable warmth still being generated from the wreck of the house. Honey came over to join Joel, sitting close up on his left side, as if contact were necessary.

'Tough night,' he told the mastiff. Honey looked at him strangely. 'Yes, I know. If I'd sent you down earlier none of this would have happened. On the other hand, they might have done you some injury, hound.'

Honey growled at him. As a self-respecting mastiff he had no wish to be called 'hound'. The girl stirred, and both man and dog craned their heads to look.

She opened her deep enigmatic eyes one at a time. Joel leaned over to brush the hair out of her face. Recognition was instantaneous. She smiled at them both, and then, with a wondering expression on her face, she murmured, 'What the devil are you doing in my dreams, my dear?' She was fast asleep again before he could work up an answer.

CHAPTER NINE

BY THREE o'clock in the morning Joel's shoulder was getting stiff, and he had lost control of the muscles in his arm. To cap the problem, the fire had been reduced to blackened embers and the night was turning chilly. Warily he stretched Kit out on the grass. She was shivering. He threw the blankets the ambulance men had left him over her, then massaged his arm. Two of the firemen left behind walked over to where he was exercising. The Harrises, father and son.

'So what now?' the father asked. He was caked with soot and water, but looked rather jaunty through it all. Not at all like the banker he is, Joel thought.

'I guess I'd better carry her up to my house,' said Joel. 'As soon as I can get some muscles working here.'

'That's crazy,' young Ed contributed. 'That's more than a quarter of a mile, and uphill all the way.'

'Doesn't make sense,' his father agreed. 'How about if I go across the street and get a car? This fire is about dead. I can be spared for as long as it takes to drive you up there. What say?'

'You've talked me out of it,' said Joel, chuckling. 'I was hoping that *somebody* would. She's a whole lot of woman.'

'Yeah, I noticed,' the son agreed, then blushed and ducked his head.

'So you stay here and watch those embers,' his father ordered, grinning. 'And keep an eye on that old barn. One or two sparks on the roof of that thing and it'll go up like tinder.'

'Hey, Pop, I didn't mean anything by that——'

'Don't concern yourself,' Joel interrupted. 'Any male between fourteen and seventy-five would think the same. Isn't that right, Mr Harris?'

'Yes, but don't tell my wife I said so. I'll get the car.'

The vehicle turned out to be a Continental, and the ride up the hill was comfortable, warm, and brief. Joel sat in the back seat with Kitty's head on his lap; Honey took advantage of the free ride, and bulked in the front seat, towering over the nervous driver.

'Come in and have one for the road,' Joel offered. The other man helped him extract himself and Kitty from the back seat and followed along to the door. 'Forgot my keys,' Joel apologised as he rang the doorbell and banged on the knocker. After what seemed to be an hour of waiting, lights flicked on in the hall, and the door opened cautiously.

'Now see here,' Carswell said sternly, then recognised whom he was addressing. 'Oh—you, Mr Carmody! I thought you were upstairs in bed!'

'Good to see you, Carswell.' It was a hearty greeting for three o'clock in the morning, from a burden-bearer who looked as if he had wrestled with a black bear—and lost.

'Er—— Yes.' Carswell held the door wide and stood aside as the three of them crossed the threshold, but his nose could not help but wrinkle.

'Bringing Miss Anderson back home,' Joel explained. The hall was poorly lighted, hiding the fact that the butler's face had just turned white. 'Help me upstairs with her, Harris. And Carswell, we'll both be down for a drink in a moment. Set something out on the sideboard.'

'Yes—yes, sir,' the butler said with a sigh. He watched the two of them climb the stairs. As soon as they were around the bend he hared off to the library, poured himself a generous brandy and soda, and threw it all down the back of his throat. All that and hardly changing the level in the soda siphon one iota. He remembered too well the day that little Mary had managed to lose herself, and Miss Anderson had commanded a search! 'Oh my!' he groaned, and doubled his medicinal draught.

Upstairs in the bedroom that Kitty had previously used Bill Harris showed unplumbed domestic depths as he stripped off the covers, fluffed up the pillows, and smoothed the sheets. Joel stretched Kitty out as gently as he could, and pulled the blankets up to cover her. She turned on her side away from them the moment she felt the warmth. A smile crept across her face, but she did not awaken. The two men stood admiring for a moment, then Joel said, 'Let's go down, shall we?'

Carswell had already fled to the back of the house before the two arrived. 'Brandy?' Joel offered. 'Or brandy? My man evidently didn't think we'd want anything else.'

'Brandy will do fine.'

Bill Harris settled back wearily in one of the overstuffed chairs. Joel poured two tulip glasses, handed one over, and walked to the window. Only a momentary glow showed from where the farmhouse had been. 'Looks to be out,' he commented as he came over and sat down.

'Done by kids?' Bill Harris asked.

'I don't know,' Joel returned. 'It's hard to tell what kids will do these days.'

'I know.' Bill Harris sighed. 'That was a fool stunt our kids pulled, trashing her house. I don't suppose they would have done it if we of the so-called older generation hadn't been so willing to listen to rumours and gossip among ourselves about it. Adolescent ears are pretty big. We types tend to forget that. It—you—gave me quite a shock. You know, there are a lot of people in the subdivision who've used every cent they own to buy into the place, and are clinging by their fingernails.

Still, the girl has a great deal of right on her side. And a couple of days ago she *did* come over and meet with us at the Community Center. She didn't say much, but she *did* listen. If only she weren't so bitter! Do you think there's any chance she might——?'

'Hard to tell,' mused Joel as he stared into the half-empty glass. 'She's a difficult woman to figure out.'

'Aren't they all?' Bill Harris chuckled. 'I've been married for twenty-nine years. Well, I've got to get back.'

Joel finished his glass and stood up. 'This volunteer fire-fighting,' he asked. 'Why?'

'Why?' The older man reflected as he finished his own brandy. 'I guess I could say public service, or social significance. But the truth of the matter is that it's lots of fun. Adventure without leaving home. The only trouble is that I'm getting too old for it. Even being up all night with a fire is no excuse for not being at my desk at nine o'clock. Well, I suppose if it were the bank's property that burned, excuses might be accepted. If you intend to stay in these parts, Mr Carmody——'

'Joel. My friends call me Joel.'

'Bill. And I'm glad to be a friend of yours.' The two of them exchanged handclasps. 'As I was saying, if you plan to remain in these parts the fire district could surely use you.'

'I would have thought, fifteen days ago, that I couldn't get out of New England fast enough,' Joel commented. 'But now—well, you might very well see me in the crowd, Bill. That is, if my wife will let me.'

Bill Harris threw back his head and laughed. 'Typical reaction,' he said when he regained control, 'but I didn't even realise you were married.'

'I'm not,' said Joel. 'Not today. But ask me again two weeks from now, and we'll see.' They were still chuckling together as he showed his neighbour to the door.

Moments later he walked slowly back up the stairs, Honey close behind him. It was a night for rule-breaking; the dog had done much to preserve that wonderful woman. One night in the house wouldn't upset the apple cart. The pair of them ghosted into Kitty's room. Honey chose the throw rug at the foot of her bed and curled up. Joel tested all three of the chairs, selected the most comfortable one, and in a moment he too was fast asleep, his head thrown back on the antimacassar. And the girl who was the centre of all this hullabaloo slept on without any idea of what had happened during the night.

There was a joy to waking up completely refreshed. Kitty threw back the covers and stretched. Her legs felt stiff, disused. But the sun was shining, a pair of finches were squabbling at her window, and the world smelled fresh and clean. Only two things nagged. This was not her own bed, and the head of a gargoyle was hanging over its foot. She blinked three times, the sure magic charm to make gargoyles go away. Instead it opened its mouth on a cavern of teeth and whined at her. Some memories returned.

What am I doing in Joel's house? she asked herself. And why is Honey staring at me like that? The dog whined, then dashed for the door. Kitty could hear his massive feet slamming down on each of the stair treads, and the stirring of other noises below.

Mrs Wright was the first to arrive—Greeks bearing gifts? On her tray coffee steamed in a sizeable mug. 'I only need that slightly less than a blood transfusion,' Kitty told her. Sara set the tray down on Kitty's knees.

'Ham, eggs, toast.' She demonstrated by lifting the covers from the various dishes.

'I can't eat all that!' Kitty protested. Sara, busy fluffing the pillows behind her, disagreed.

'After all that excitement last night, you ought to be able to eat a horse, Katherine! Now come on, dig in. Or do I have to go down and tell Himself that you won't co-operate?'

'Good lord, no!' Kitty almost upset the tray in her agitation. 'I don't want that man within ten miles of me. Twenty, if I had the choice. I think I'd break out in hives if he were close by!'

Sara smiled and shook her head. 'I may never come to understand the younger generation,' she said. 'You must be a mass of skin eruptions by now. He brought you home and then sat up all night with you, over in that chair by your bed. In fact he didn't want to leave at all, but about twenty minutes ago the police arrived, and he had to talk to them.'

'It's just as well he's gone,' Kitty muttered. 'I've a thing or two to say to him too. What right does he have to come over to my house and kidnap me? It had to be that, you know—kidnapping! I took a couple of sleeping pills before I dozed off, and the next thing I know I wake up over here again. That man needs some considerable straightening out!' She dabbed at her eyes with the corner of the sheet.

'Sara?' she began.

'What, dear?'

'Is it possible to——?'

'To what, love?'

'To hate a man so terribly you could spit, and love him at the same time?'

Sara gave her a curious look. 'That's the way you see it?'

'That's the way I see it,' Kitty snapped. 'I don't understand him. I don't understand me. And that's all I can eat.' Her voice softened as she looked up at Mrs Wright. 'You know, I think a great deal of you, Sara.

It's just that arrogant opinionated devil that I can't stand!'

'Yes, I can see that.' There was a lilt of laughter behind the cook's statement. 'And if you're finished here, why don't you get out of bed and come down?'

'But I—I don't seem to have any clothes,' Kitty reported after she had bounced out of bed and toured the wardrobes. 'Do you suppose someone could go down to my house and get me something to wear?'

'I doubt it.' Sara picked up the tray, and started for the door. 'As far as I know everything in the house was burned to a crisp.'

'*What?* What did you say?'

'I said,' the housekeeper said very slowly, as if talking to a dimwit, 'your house burned to the ground last night, and if it hadn't been for Joel, young lady, you might have burned down with it. Got himself some nasty burns while he was at it.'

'But I——' Kitty began.

'I know, child. He loves you very much, you know.'

'But I——'

'And then he sat up in that chair by your bed for the rest of the night, and——'

'Oh lord! I——'

'Love him too, don't you? Anybody can see that. If only the pair of you weren't so darn stubborn things would be a lot easier around these parts.' And without another word of explanation Sara headed for the kitchen.

All of which explained why Kitty, still dressed in her long cotton nightgown, but covered by a borrowed robe, walked hesitantly into the drawing-room downstairs only moments later, her hair full of curls and her eyes full of hopes and aspirations.

Joel was sitting on the chair directly in front of the door, stripped to the waist, while a doctor poked and prodded at his burns and bruises. There were a round

dozen other men in the room, but Kitty had eyes only
for him. She strode across the thick rug and tapped him
on the shoulder. 'Joel Carmody,' she said in her most
conciliatory tone—and only then realised that the room
was full of strangers. 'Oh, lord!' she muttered, and
would have fled had not she been so loaded with a guilty
conscience. 'I ought to——'

He squirmed around in his chair and looked up at her.
'Yes, why don't you sit down, Kit?' He gestured around
the room. Kitty felt as if she had shrunk to the size of
an elf. The room was full of men, most of them bulky
and uniformed. And here I am in my nightgown again,
she mourned to herself. Her cheeks blushed as she tried
to move behind Joel's chair, hoping to become invisible.
'I need to tell you something privately——' she
whispered.

'And all these men have something to tell you,' he
interrupted. 'The gentleman in the middle there, in the
blue suit, is Mr Medeiros, the Bristol County district
attorney,' Joel continued. 'Lieutenant Frankel you know.
These other gentlemen are from the district attorney's
strike force. Oh, and the man on the end there is Mr
Eddy, the editor of the local newspaper. Go ahead, make
your complaint.'

'I don't—have a complaint,' she muttered.

'I don't believe that,' he returned. 'I wish the hell I
did. Go ahead.'

A moment of anger grew, flashed, and was ex-
tinguished. This is the day when I'm not going to lose
my temper, Kitty told herself firmly. 'I'll go when I'm
ready,' she said through gritted teeth. Joel turned around
in his chair and glared at her. 'All right,' she muttered,
'I'm ready.' She squared her shoulders and walked
around in front of him.

'Joel Carmody,' she said very softly, very solemnly.
'Yes?'

'I love you very much. I *do* trust you.'

He didn't respond the way she had expected. The doctor put his hand in the wrong place and Joel shivered. 'Well, it will take more than a statement to make me believe it,' he said. She could hear his teeth grate as he tried to keep from groaning.

Kitty looked around the room at all those huge men staring at her, took a deep breath to settle her nerves, and almost fell back into a chair...

'It might help you to know,' said Mr Eddy, 'that my paper's headlines this week will read "Heroic Tycoon Saves Hopkins Neck Girl".'

'You mean me?' she gasped. He nodded. 'Well——' Kitty was working her way up to another good mad, 'here I've apologised and said something that I swore I would never say to any man, and—— '

'And very prettily done too,' Joel interjected.

'And then you just sit there and grin at me like some—like——' The words were choked off by her choler. 'Why, I—I'll bet he didn't do any such a thing, or if he did it was just to spite me!'

And so much for all those dreams, Kitty told herself. He doesn't care a hill of beans. Not even a *little* bit. I'll bet if I stripped and danced around him and fell into his lap he'd make some sarcastic remark. Damn the man. You've no one to blame but yourself, the voice of her conscience interrupted. You dreamed it all and then pronounced it all true. How stupid can one girl get?

Everyone in the room was staring at Joel. Glumly, Kitty joined them. He shrugged. 'She slept through the whole thing,' he explained, choosing his words carefully. 'Sleeping pills or something.'

'Oh my,' the editor said. And then in a higher laughter-filled pitch, 'Oh my!' His eyes crinkled. 'I promised my wife I'd never stoop so low, but I think when I get back to the office I'll change that to read "Prince rescues Sleeping Beauty"!'

Kitty stamped her foot, forgetting about the thick rug, and glared at them all. Speaking very slowly, as if to an audience of idiots, she said, 'There must be *one* of you who has all his marbles. Whoever you are, would you kindly explain what's going on?'

'In just a minute,' the district attorney told her. 'We're waiting for Miss—ah, here she is.' The door closed gently as Faith Latimore came breezily into the room.

'My, you're up, sleepyhead!'

'Faith, they're trying to tell me that my house——' Kitty began.

'Burned to the ground,' her lawyer assured her. 'But we have insurance, if you remember. You're one lucky lady. If Mr Carmody and his dog hadn't been out and about late last night, you might have become a well-done farmer. Did you thank him?'

Kitty turned to look over her shoulder at Joel's face. His mouth was half open, and those teeth reminded her of Honey's. 'You could have explained it before I made such a fool of myself,' she said.

'Yes. But unfortunately I was all tied up with the doctor.' He struggled, with the doctor's help, to slide his arms back into his shirt.

'Try to imagine me as the good guy,' he suggested wistfully. 'I know it will take some stretching of your imagination, but it might help us all in the long run. Go ahead with the explanations, Mr Medeiros.'

'Well,' the district attorney said finally, 'working on the theory that today's heroes are tomorrow's forgotten men, maybe we'd better hurry along. Now let's see here. Lieutenant Frankel?'

'First, the arson case.' The lieutenant stood up, using the occasional table as a podium for his briefcase-load of papers. 'The fire was set by the use of gasoline. Two empty cans of it were found thrown away at the scene of the crime. The fire assessment team and the State police laboratory confirm this. When the fire was noted, a road-block was established on the road to Hopkins Neck. At approximately ten minutes after the fire broke out, we apprehended five men in a four-wheel-drive truck belonging to Mr James Randolph.'

'That's the first selectman?' editor Eddy prodded.

'The very same. The driver of the truck was a Mr Francis Randolph, the son of the owner. The other four passengers were juveniles, so their names will not be revealed. In the back of the truck were two full five-gallon cans of gasoline. The owner of the Shell station at the corner of Main and Pleasant tells us that Mr Randolph—the younger man—paid for four such cans of gas at his station yesterday afternoon. Fingerprints on the empty cans are those of Randolph and two of the juveniles.'

'It certainly looks open and shut,' the district attorney commented. 'Motive?'

'I—had an—argument with him at the supermarket yesterday,' Kit offered.

'I rather suspect there's a bigger motive than that,' Faith Latimore said. 'There's a related crime, Mr Medeiros.'

'What might that be, counsellor?'

'Well, sir, it is definitely falsification of public records. From there it might well grow into malfeasance in office.'

'And related to this case?'

'Closely.'

'All right, tell me about it.'

'To begin with, there are a series of shore-front lots developed by Sheering Construction. Forty-six lots, to be exact. Percolation tests were made prior to construction. All the results were certified, allowing the building to proceed. If you'll look at a few of these.'

Faith pulled out a series of official sheets and scattered them in front of the district attorney.

'I'm afraid I'm not expert enough——' he protested.

'No need for that,' Faith told him. 'They've been analysed by experts. To be exact, twenty of these certificates are accurate, the other twenty-six are repetitive. In other words, the same figures for the first twenty were re-used for the remaining lots. All forty-six were certified.'

'By whom?'

'By Mr James Randolph, the first selectman.'

'Oh hell!' the district attorney grumbled. 'We've an election coming up. Randolph is a party hack, but the only one who can guarantee the Northport vote. You're sure of this?'

'Positive, sir. It would appear that Mr Randolph conspired with an unnamed financial supporter to illegally build the subdivision, profiting to the tune of one hundred thousand dollars.'

'Counsellor, are you willing to work with my people on this?'

'I am.'

'Then we'll proceed before the grand jury as soon as you're ready. Now, if you'll excuse me, there's other business in Bristol County that I must see to.'

There was a vast shuffling of feet, and an exodus that might well have paralleled the Red Sea affair. In fact, within minutes the drawing-room was empty, save for Kitty and Joel. Kitty fought between the need to move and the comfort of staying where she was. And then John walked in and settled things in her mind. She pulled herself out her chair and started for the door.

'No, Katherine,' both men said at the same time. Confused, she looked back and forth between them. It was startling to see that John was completely under control, so neat, and yet so sombre. 'We have a family matter to discuss,' said John.

'That lets me out,' Kitty retorted, and headed for the door again, only to be trapped as Joel grabbed at her wrist and pulled her back.

'No, this concerns the family—and you, Kit.'

'I don't see why,' she muttered. 'I think I've had enough of the Carmody family already.'

'We haven't treated you too well,' said Joel in a surprisingly soft voice. 'I have to agree. But we need to talk. You heard Faith——'

'You know my lawyer that well?'

'Of course I do. When she needed a detective, I hired one.'

'Well, you've got a nerve!' She glared at him, ignoring his brother. The man has more turns and bends than a rattlesnake! she told herself indignantly. And then another thought struck her. 'An unnamed conspirator,' she said flatly.

'Exactly. That's what we have to talk about,' John contributed.

'An unnamed conspirator,' Kitty murmured. She turned quickly in Joel's direction. 'You?'

'That's what I like,' he returned. 'Always willing to believe the worst of anybody, Kit?'

She almost answered him in the heat of anger. Two weeks ago she would have, she knew. And why the hesitation now? For no good reason? Or because she had proof positive, and didn't *want* to believe it? Her heart cried *not* to believe! 'No,' she sighed. 'Not always.'

'Why don't you two let me tell this part of the tale?' John interrupted. 'Before you both come to blows, I mean. Kit?'

'I'm listening. But I'm not prepared to believe a great deal.'

'It takes money to make money,' John said in a quiet voice the like of which Kitty had never heard. 'In this case the Carmody Corporation was the source of that money. Somebody in the executive office of the corporation embezzled two hundred and fifty thousand dollars, and invested most of it in this get-rich-quick scheme. The unnamed conspirator.'

'So does he have a name?' It wasn't possible for Kitty to stand still for this. She had spent a long year looking for the answer that John seemed to have. Her nervous energy was at its peak; the only trouble was that she really didn't want to hear the name! For fear, of course, that it would be the name of the man—oh hell, she told herself, admit it, stupid—of the man she loved!

'There is a name,' John continued. He opened the drawer in the side of the table, pulled out more papers, and spread them out. 'These,' he said, 'are the vouchers on which the false payments were made.' Kitty dropped into a chair to examine them.

She could understand hardly anything about the codes and accounting symbols. But down at the bottom, where the printed form said 'Authorised by', things became very simple. All of the vouchers were endorsed by 'J Carmody', in a sprawling hand that could not be mistaken.

'J Carmody,' she mused. 'You, John?'

'No, not me.'

'Then it must be J Carmody, you, Joel!'

'And not me either,' said Joel. 'You'll note that all those vouchers were signed weeks before I came up here from Kentucky.'

'Well, I don't understand it,' she said, shaking her head in puzzlement. 'There are only two J Carmodys, and they're both in this room!'

The words hung in the air for a moment, vibrating.
'Not quite true,' John responded reluctantly. 'You forget
my wife.'

'Your wife? Oh lord—Jessica Carmody! Jessica!'

'Just so, Katherine.' Joel was up from his chair and
around behind her. One hand came to rest on her hip.
She leaned back against him, suddenly empty of thought,
emotion.

'Jessica,' she murmured, and leaned back against his
warmth and strength. 'Oh, Joel, I've made a terrible
mess of everything, haven't I?'

An hour later they gathered again, this time in the
kitchen. John and Joel and Kitty and Mary, all seated
around the table. Mrs Wright had left them a meal of
cold cuts and had gone home 'to see to my niece, who's
visiting. These young ones can't do a thing for themselves these days.' Or so Sara said when she went out of
the door.

'A very young niece?' Kitty asked Joel as the cook
disappeared down the front steps.

'About your age,' he agreed, and led her back to the
kitchen.

'So...' she hesitated to ask, but felt she had to '...so
where is Jessica?'

'At Millport sanatorium,' John told her. 'She's close
to a nervous breakdown. She stands in great danger of
being indicted. But despite all this, she's still my wife.
If I hadn't been such a weakling months ago she might
never have gone off the rails as she did. Now I intend
to stand by her, get her the best defence lawyer I can
find——'

'Faith,' Kitty suggested. 'Faith Latimore. The finest
you can get. Will it be a hard case?'

'That depends,' said Joel. 'The money she took
illegally is actually family money. We could refuse to

prosecute. But you, Kit, you represent the other danger. Do *you* want to prosecute? You could invalidate the land sale, put the entire subdivision in jeopardy, put Jessica and Randolph and probably half a dozen others in jail. All that is in your power. And Jessica is this person you've been looking for for a long time. You've got her right where you want her! All you have to do is say the word.'

'Yes, I understand all that,' she said softly. 'She hurt the Anderson family very much. I have to think this over, all of it.' It was hard to keep the quaver out of her voice, or the tears from her eyes. It isn't fair, she told herself. I shouldn't have to choose between them!

'And when you've done your thinking,' said Joel, 'regardless of what decision you make, there's something you and I have to talk about.'

'Yes,' said Kitty. She stood up. The baby smiled at her. The two men, their faces drawn, rose in courtesy. Honey, who had been lying on the floor by the table, got up and went with her. As far as the library she went, and closed the door behind her, shutting the dog out in the corridor. She didn't realise that the latch had not clicked shut. She had a great deal to think about.

Kitty walked over to the one window that looked down on the site of her house. Her father's house. The home her grandfather had expected would be the seat of the Anderson family for generations to come. Through the branches of the trees along the brook she could see the flame-blackened land. But it was only a house, her conscience cried at her. Only a house. Robert and I are the last Andersons. She fingered the letter in her pocket. The letter that had been delivered to her days late by a post office which did not quite know where she was. The letter, finally, from Robert.

'You won't believe it,' he wrote, 'but I've found a quieter, gentler place. I won't be coming home, dear Kit.

My thanks and my love will follow you wherever you go.' There was no return address, but the superscription on the simple page read, 'The Monastery of the Dominican Brothers'. And so Robert had found his refuge, and all her hating had been in vain.

And the subdivision and all its families? wondered Kitty. All those people waiting down there to see what I intend to do? Misguided people, perhaps, but they did not deserve to be thrown out of their homes, torn from their land. There's the secret—torn from *their* land. Can anything be done for them? The simple honest fact remained that they were polluting the land, and there was no legal way Kitty Anderson could do anything about that. Unless Joel——? Joel, the man who could do anything?

The Randolphs, father and son, betraying the public trust for money, attempted murder, arson? I might forgive, but the law will not. They're beyond me and my hatred, she thought.

Jessica Carmody? The smooth, suave lady with the disturbed life. Her husband intends to defend her, whatever she's done. I wish I had somebody who thought of me in that way! Jessica Carmody. Jessica Carmody. The name echoed with each step she took. Jessica Carmody. She walked the narrow perimeter of the room, her eyes unfocused.

Kitty almost fell over the answer. It was on top of a mahogany reading stand, set up to the proper height so one could read while standing, equipped with rollers to allow for movement around the room. And there, resting open on its inclined top, was a huge old copy of the Holy Bible, King James version. The big old book lay open to Paul's letter to the Romans, Chapter Twelve. The capital letters that began each paragraph were skilfully embossed in blue and gold. And the words leaped out at her from the page. 'For it is written, vengeance is mine; I will repay, saith the Lord.'

Kitty clutched at the desk for support, feeling as if a terrible burden had just been lifted from her shoulders. Her legs protested. She slipped down to the floor, still clutching at the leg of the desk. The dog pawed at the door from outside, and the latch let go. In a minute Honey was in the room and at her side. The big mastiff did what might seem an impossible thing: he sat and wagged all at the same time. The big rough tongue came over and licked her patrician nose.

'All right, all right!' Kitty, her heart unburdened, laughed—weak, but still laughter. The dog wiggled a little closer. 'So all right,' she told him, 'I admit it—I like dogs. But not now with the licking, please, I'm so tired.'

The open door was a fatal attraction to another traveller. Little Mary Carmody had somehow escaped from her baby-watchers, and came down the hall on hands and knees. Now she manoeuvred through the door, having a little trouble with the raised threshold. A moment's hard work brought her up to her chubby little feet, and she wavered across the length of the long narrow room and stopped an inch or two away from the half-sleepy woman and the watchful dog.

'Mama,' the baby said with a self-satisfied tone, and plunked herself down in Kitty's lap. Kitty moved a couple of inches to get more comfortable. The child wiggled and squirmed until she was in just the right place. 'So all right,' Kitty Anderson, the town grouch, murmured drowsily. 'I could be wrong on both counts. I like dogs *and* kids.' And Joel too, she reminded herself thoughtfully. But I can't marry him if he doesn't love me. He might want me to warm his bed, or to look after his niece, or to keep his house—but he doesn't love me, so

I can't marry him. Besides, he's never asked me, has he? So no more castles in the clouds, Katherine Anderson. Feet on the floor, firm but polite, and——! At which point all three of them fell asleep.

CHAPTER TEN

WHEN she awoke from her afternoon nap three days later, Kitty knew something was wrong. The house was absolutely silent; not a bird call, a child noise, a dog whimper. And Joel was sitting back in the chair next to her bed. The day was hot, one of the last 'dog-days' of August. She was very thankful that she had only stripped off her dress. Armour plate was more likely her need around the multi-handed Joel Carmody, but a full slip would have to do.

'Good morning,' she hurried to say, trying to get in the first shot. 'And no, I don't intend to marry you. And I don't care how many times more you ask me!'

'That's not a very nice attitude, Katherine.' Those big green eyes watched her like a hawk, despite the pleasant smile on his face. 'Now, as we were saying——'

'Do we *have* to?' she pleaded.

'We *have* to. You've dodged and ducked for three days. You've been tired, you've been hungry, you've had a headache.'

'I can feel one coming on now,' she interjected.

'Good. I've got aspirin here, Tylenol over there on the bureau. A sandwich if you're hungry. You can't possibly be sleepy after the nap you've had.' He glared at her. 'What else?'

'Nothing,' she said with a gusty sigh. 'I can't think of anything else.'

'Good. Now, I don't intend to ask you again to marry me. The time for asking is over.'

'You don't?' So he's finally gotten the message, she told herself. Just when I've come to the conclusion that it's the wrong answer. But if I *did* marry him he'd have me under his thumb day and night! Well, maybe the nights might not be so bad, but—dear lord, how it hurts to fall in love!

'Now this is strictly business,' he said. 'You've agreed not to prosecute in any portion of this affair, right?'

She nodded.

'Mind telling me why?'

'Because——' Because I don't *want* to tell you, you arrogant rotten man!

'Because? What kind of an answer is that?'

'Oh, leave me alone! This isn't the Inquisition!' Besides, what do you want from me besides blood, she thought. I should stand up and do a Greta Garbo, the 'world is well lost for love of you'? You big hulking bully! 'I need something to drink!'

'Of course you do. Here—nice fresh spring water.' He passed her the glass. 'You know that I know what your trouble is?' The smile was back on his face, and her alarms all went off at once.

'You can't possibly know!' she shouted at him.

'See? You're giving yourself away,' he told her. 'Look, girl. You love my dog, you love my niece, and you love me. Why don't you admit it?'

'You tell awful lies,' she grumbled. 'I thought we weren't going to talk about that any more. I know what you want. You're looking for a nice biddable girl who'll look after the kid for you—at a cheap wage! Someone who'll feed your dogs and mend your socks and warm your bed. Well, I'm not nice and I'm not biddable and I—wipe that grin off your face, darn you! Don't think you can pull the wool oh, you know!'

Joel settled back in his chair and smiled again. 'It's going to be a wonderful life, Katherine, if we can ever get it started. But you're right. Today we're going to talk about sewers. After that, no more talk. How's that grab you?'

'It's about time.' Kitty took a deep breath and was immediately both contrite and suspicious. 'I *do* like your dog. I could probably like your niece, if she weren't *your* niece. I mean if she——'

'I know what you mean. Now—sewers. Are you ready for this?'

'I'm ready. Do your darnedest.'

'As you remember, Kit, twenty out of the forty-six houses in the subdivision passed the perc tests. Now, there's a solution for the rest. You listening?'

'Of course I'm listening. I promised those people we'd do everything we can to help them.' We? How did that word get in the conversation?

'OK. There's a company up in Braintree that makes tiny sewer plants. Plants that take up one house lot, but can absorb and process fifty or sixty houses' sewerage, and discharge into a single leaching field.'

'You'd better spell that out,' she sighed. 'My head really aches.' Joel handed her an aspirin to go with her glass of water.

'What it amounts to is this. We get two of these mini-sewer plants, and set them on a house lot somewhat lower than the subdivision. Then we install sewer pipes from all the houses which are on lots that didn't pass the perc test. Total cost, about six hundred dollars per house.'

'I'll bet it would smell. And it would work?'

'Guaranteed. It's already been tried in a dozen places, and is totally odourless. Now, in consideration of our involvement the Carmody Corporation will pay the costs, but——'

'I just knew there would be a *but*,' Kitty said suspiciously. 'But what?'

'Well, as it happens, the only house lot that meets our requirements, the one which can pass a perc test and have plenty of room for two sewer plants—it happens to belong to Katherine Anderson.'

'So I'll donate it,' she decided quickly. 'A free gift. Now, we've settled all your problems, I have only one question and then you can go away!'

'One thing at a time. What's the question?'

'What about Jessica?'

'Funny you should ask.' Joel shook his head and frowned. 'John tells me that the doctors actually found something physically wrong with her. She's under treatment. Carmody Corporation will not press charges. John says he loves her, and I almost believe it. Anyway, he plans to devote all his time and attention to getting her out from under.'

'I'm really glad to hear that, Joel.' Her fingers had been flexing in her lap. Now she stilled them. 'I was *so* sure that Jessica would——'

'Be a bone of contention between you and me?'

'There isn't any you and me!' she yelled at him. 'Now, could you kindly go away?'

'No, we still have this other problem,' he laughed. 'I want to marry you, Mary wants me to marry you, Sara wants me to marry you. I even took a census in the kennels, and the dogs want me to marry you. That was a hundred per cent vote, by the way.'

'Don't *do* that,' she insisted. 'We weren't going to talk about marriage! Who would want to marry an arrogant—fellow like you? All you want me for is—lust—that's what I think! No, thank you. And I don't intend to fall in love with your niece. She's a nice kid. She deserves better than you. But I don't like her *that* much!' And that first part, her conscience dictated, is a bunch of malarkey. You'd love to have him lust for your body! Stop kidding yourself, Katherine!

'Stop yelling,' he told her. 'There's nobody home to hear. I sent them all away for the day. And I *don't* want you just to be Mary's mother, Katherine.' He stood up and came over to the bed, leaning over with those big wolf-teeth gleaming at her. 'I want you for your lovely body, for your mean temper, and for your marvellous soul.'

'Well, you can't have me,' she snapped. 'I'm not on sale this week. Or next either! Now is that the last word on the subject?' It wasn't much of an argument, but he was getting closer, and her defences were collapsing before he even attacked.

'That's the last word,' Joel agreed. He's not to be trusted, Kitty told herself as he sat down on the edge of the bed. She moved carefully away, checking carefully to find an escape route. His eyes followed hers. He got up, stretched, walked over to the door and shot the bolt—then started to take off his shirt and tie.

'What are you doing?' she gasped. The first signs of panic were building up in her, and it was hard to keep her senses about her.

'No more words,' he said ominously. His trousers followed his shirt. Kitty turned her back on him and pulled her knees up to her stomach. His shoes clumped on the floor, and she ducked her head.

'Don't you dare!' she yelled at him when the mattress sank under his weight. 'Don't you——'

'Dare' was to have been the last word, but he did dare indeed. A finger tangled in her long golden hair and pulled her over backwards on the bed. He was at her lips before she could scream Jack Robinson. In fact she knew she didn't want to scream Jack Robinson, or anything else. She had known it from the very first moment. He tasted so good, so warm, so—tasty. When his mouth moved on and his teeth nibbled at her earlobe she managed one pro forma protest. 'What are you doing?'

'No more words,' he whispered into her ear. Somehow she had lost her slip. It meant a great deal. Her bra was a sometime thing, a wisp of black lace worn more for decoration than support. She squirmed, trying to get away from him, but one of his bare legs came over her, pinning her in position, and her bra disappeared.

Somebody was moaning, a wild feminine moan that ricocheted off the walls and came back to run up Kitty's spine. Somebody was feasting on her breasts, and the impulse to squirm came back—but in Joel's direction. She felt his weight as it came down on her pelvis. Not a punishing weight, but a fulsome challenge. A string of kisses started at her navel and chased themselves up and over her breasts again. Every nerve in her body was attuned to the invasion, wanting more, groping blindly. She closed her eyes. Hands were running down across the tiny swell of her stomach, and jumping down into the valley between her thighs. Her mind slipped completely out of her control. 'Oh, lord!' she moaned.

And then suddenly she was cold and overheated at the same time, and alone. Her body jerked a few times, looking for its wonderful tormentor—who was no longer there. Carefully Kitty opened one eye. Joel was sitting on the edge of the bed, dressing.

'You you can't do this to me!' she shrieked at him.

'Can't I? I don't think I've ever met a woman who was turned on so quickly—and so thoroughly!'

'Did you not?' she spat at him bitterly. 'I suppose you've had lots of practice!'

'Who, me? Not a chance.' He looked over his shoulder and gave her a friendly smile. 'But when I was in the Army the men used to come back to the barracks and tell me all about it!'

'You—rotten man,' she gasped. 'You can't leave me like this!'

'Yes, I can,' he retorted. 'It isn't easy, but I can.'

'All right,' she capitulated, 'what's the bargain?'

'Marriage,' he said. 'I'm almost a virgin, and I can't be had any other way.'

'Joel Carmody, do you really love me?' she demanded.

'I've told you a thousand times. Of course I do.'

'I don't believe I heard you say it a single time! You think I'm some sort of pushover, don't you?'

He stood up and zippered his trousers. 'No, I don't, Kit. I think I'm the only man in the world who can turn you on like this. And there's no need for you to go through all the rest of your life, suffering for something which I can provide oh, so easily. You hear me, woman?'

'I hear you,' she said almost under her breath. All her hatreds and inhibitions had disappeared at that moment. All the joys that had been suppressed for so long came back into flower. 'Well——' she said hesitantly '—I guess there's nothing else I can do but marry you.'

'Why?' he snapped.

'Because I love you, you fool. And you're going to get everything you deserve!'

'I've been praying for that,' he laughed as he bent down to kiss her.

'Well, while I'm waiting do you think could you pass me that sandwich you said you had? I'm awful hungry.'

Joel worked up a glare, but even Kitty could see it was a fake. He wasn't faking, though, as he kicked off his shoes and began to unzip his trousers again. She shivered in anticipation, and decided the sandwich could wait.

They were married two days later in the office of the justice of the peace on Main Street, in Northport. Mary was the flower girl, wobbling unsupported in front of the bride and groom, until she plopped down on her round little bottom and laughed herself to tears. John gave the bride away, Sara Wright threw confetti on the steps, and Honey, waiting in the back of the car, wondered what all the fuss was about!

HISTORICAL

CHRISTMAS

STORIES · 1991

Bring back heartwarming memories of Christmas past,
with Historical Christmas Stories 1991, a collection of
romantic stories by three popular authors:

Christmas Yet To Come
by Lynda Trent
A Season of Joy
by Caryn Cameron
Fortune's Gift
by DeLoras Scott
A perfect Christmas gift!

Don't miss these heartwarming stories, available in December at your favorite
retail outlet. Or order your copy now by sending your name, address, zip or
postal code, along with a check or money order for $4.99 (please do not send
cash), plus 75¢ postage and handling ($1.00 in Canada), payable to Harlequin
Books to:

In the U.S.

3010 Walden Ave.
P.O. Box 1396
Buffalo, NY 14269-1396

In Canada

P.O. Box 609
Fort Erie, Ontario
L2A 5X3

Please specify book title with your order.
Canadian residents add applicable federal and provincial taxes.

XM-91-2

"INDULGE A LITTLE" SWEEPSTAKES

HERE'S HOW THE SWEEPSTAKES WORKS

NO PURCHASE NECESSARY

To enter each drawing, complete the appropriate Official Entry Form or a 3" by 5" index card by hand-printing your name, address and phone number and the trip destination that the entry is being submitted for (i.e., Walt Disney World Vacation Drawing, etc.) and mailing it to: Indulge '91 Subscribers-Only Sweepstakes, P.O. Box 1397, Buffalo, New York 14269-1397.

No responsibility is assumed for lost, late or misdirected mail. Entries must be sent separately with first class postage affixed, and be received by: 9/30/91 for the Walt Disney World Vacation Drawing, 10/31/91 for the Alaskan Cruise Drawing and 11/30/91 for the Hawaiian Vacation Drawing. Sweepstakes is open to residents of the U.S. and Canada, 21 years of age or older as of 11/7/91.

For complete rules, send a self-addressed, stamped (WA residents need not affix return postage) envelope to: Indulge '91 Subscribers-Only Sweepstakes Rules, P.O. Box 4005, Blair, NE 68009.

"INDULGE A LITTLE" SWEEPSTAKES

HERE'S HOW THE SWEEPSTAKES WORKS

NO PURCHASE NECESSARY

To enter each drawing, complete the appropriate Official Entry Form or a 3" by 5" index card by hand-printing your name, address and phone number and the trip destination that the entry is being submitted for (i.e., Walt Disney World Vacation Drawing, etc.) and mailing it to: Indulge '91 Subscribers-Only Sweepstakes, P.O. Box 1397, Buffalo, New York 14269-1397.

No responsibility is assumed for lost, late or misdirected mail. Entries must be sent separately with first class postage affixed, and be received by: 9/30/91 for the Walt Disney World Vacation Drawing, 10/31/91 for the Alaskan Cruise Drawing and 11/30/91 for the Hawaiian Vacation Drawing. Sweepstakes is open to residents of the U.S. and Canada, 21 years of age or older as of 11/7/91.

For complete rules, send a self-addressed, stamped (WA residents need not affix return postage) envelope to: Indulge '91 Subscribers-Only Sweepstakes Rules, P.O. Box 4005, Blair, NE 68009.

© 1991 HARLEQUIN ENTERPRISES LTD.   DIR-RL

INDULGE A LITTLE—WIN A LOT!

Summer of '91 Subscribers-Only Sweepstakes

OFFICIAL ENTRY FORM

This entry must be received by: Nov. 30, 1991
This month's winner will be notified by: Dec. 7, 1991
Trip must be taken between: Jan. 7, 1992—Jan. 7, 1993

YES, I want to win the 3-Island Hawaiian vacation for two. I understand the prize includes round-trip airfare, first-class hotels and pocket money as revealed on the "wallet" scratch-off card.

Name _____

Address_____ Apt. _____

City _____

State/Prov. _____ Zip/Postal Code _____

Daytime phone number _____
(Area Code)

Return entries with invoice in envelope provided. Each book in this shipment has two entry coupons—and the more coupons you enter, the better your chances of winning!

© 1991 HARLEQUIN ENTERPRISES LTD.   3R-CPS

INDULGE A LITTLE—WIN A LOT!

Summer of '91 Subscribers-Only Sweepstakes

OFFICIAL ENTRY FORM

This entry must be received by: Nov. 30, 1991
This month's winner will be notified by: Dec. 7, 1991
Trip must be taken between: Jan. 7, 1992—Jan. 7, 1993

YES, I want to win the 3-Island Hawaiian vacation for two. I understand the prize includes round-trip airfare, first-class hotels and pocket money as revealed on the "wallet" scratch-off card.

Name _____

Address_____ Apt. _____

City _____

State/Prov. _____ Zip/Postal Code _____

Daytime phone number _____
(Area Code)

Return entries with invoice in envelope provided. Each book in this shipment has two entry coupons—and the more coupons you enter, the better your chances of winning!

© 1991 HARLEQUIN ENTERPRISES LTD.   3R-CPS